PEN PALS:

TOO CUTE
FOR WORDS

ESPECIALLY FOR GIRLS® Presents

PEN PALS:

TOO CUTE
FOR WORDS

by Sharon Dennis Wyeth

A YEARLING BOOK

This book is a presentation of **Especially for Girls**®, Weekly Reader Books. Weekly Reader Books offers book clubs for children from preschool through high school. For further information write to: **Weekly Reader Books,** 4343 Equity Drive, Columbus, Ohio 43228.

Published by arrangement with Dell Publishing, a division of Bantam Doubleday Dell Publishing Group, Inc. Especially for Girls and Weekly Reader are federally registered trademarks of Field Publications.

A Yearling Book
Dell Publishing
   New York

Published by
Dell Publishing
a division of
Bantam Doubleday Dell Publishing Group, Inc.
666 Fifth Avenue
New York, New York 10103

ISBN: 0-440-40225-5
Published by arrangement with Parachute Press, Inc.
Printed in the United States of America
September 1989
10   9   8   7   6   5   4   3
OPM

For Georgia

PEN PALS:

TOO CUTE
FOR WORDS

CHAPTER ONE

Dear Lisa,

Salve vixen! By now, your Latin must be good enough to translate that. How are the old Latin classes going over there at Alma Stephens Prison for Girls?

Isn't this freezing-cold weather a drag! Life here at Ard-Barf Boys Penitentiary is starting to get to me. All anybody thinks about is grades, grades, grades. I couldn't care less about grades. I hate to study, and reading textbooks is a bore. Lucky for me I like to read the newspaper. I steal all the topics for my English compositions from the Times. *And I aced a government studies exam last week because of some facts I got from the financial section. My grades are okay, thanks to the newspaper.*

> *Your pen pal,*
> *Rob*

P.S. Have I told you lately that I think you write amazing letters?

"*Salve vixen?*" drawled Palmer Durand. "What does that mean?"

Lisa put down the letter she'd been reading aloud. "It means 'Hey, foxes'!" she said, smiling.

"Only *vixen* isn't Latin," added Shanon Davis, who was kneeling on the floor, trying to make a pot of tea with her electric heating coil. "I think it's old English."

"Who cares what language it is." Lisa McGreevy sighed and stretched out on the loveseat. "I think Rob Williams is the neatest guy at Ardsley Academy. I can't wait to see him again." She pressed the letter to her heart and then slipped it into the pocket of her jeans skirt. "I'll read this again when Amy gets here."

Palmer tossed her blond curls and looked away. It was annoying to hear how well things were going with Lisa's pen pal when Palmer was so unhappy with her own. Feeling somewhat irritated with everyone and everything, she suddenly snapped at Shanon. "That water is never going to boil."

"Sure it will," said Shanon cheerfully. "Just wait and see!" Nothing was going to spoil her mood. The teapot had arrived that very morning—a present from her mom. And she'd gotten a letter from her own pen pal, Mars.

"What did Mars say in his letter?" Lisa asked, sitting up on her elbow.

Shanon blushed and reached into the pocket of her long gray sweater. "I was going to wait until Amy got here."

"Amy won't mind," Lisa assured her. "When she gets here, you can read it a second time."

Shanon smiled. "Okay. Sometimes reading it out loud the second time is better anyway. . . ."

2

Dear Shanon,

My pen-holder business is going extremely well. Thanks for saying it's a good idea. It's a totally useless invention— but that's why people like it. Rob, John, and Simmie were being real buzz crushers about it, but now that I've sold twelve of these things they've become believers. Sorry I haven't sent you yours yet. I will, as soon as I perfect it.

Sincerely,

Mars

"Incredible!" Lisa said enthusiastically.

"It *is* pretty nice," Shanon agreed. "He practically says that I inspired his pen-holder invention."

"Sounds totally stupid to me," Palmer said flatly. "What's a pen holder anyway?"

"Don't you remember how Mars described it in his last letter?" Shanon said. "It's simply a strip of dyed leather wrapped around a pen like a handle! You can carry your pen around like a suitcase!"

Palmer rolled her eyes. "That's ridiculous."

"It's a joke invention," Lisa countered. "Mars knows that. He *told* Shanon that it was totally useless."

"If it's totally useless, why invent it in the first place?" Palmer insisted.

"If the whole world thought that way there wouldn't be any fun things in the stores," Lisa pointed out.

"I think the tea water is ready," Shanon announced, bending over her teapot. "My mom sent me some peppermint teabags. Does everybody want some?"

"I'm going to Germaine's room," said Palmer. "She makes instant coffee with her heating coil."

"Just a minute," said Lisa. "What about the letter you got from John?"

"Yes," Shanon said. "Why don't you read it to us?"

"I can't find it," Palmer hedged. "I stuck it in one of my biology books and it must've gotten lost or something."

"But you *will* read it to us when you find it?" Lisa persisted.

"I will if it's so important to you," Palmer mumbled. Two red spots appeared on her cheeks. "I'll see you later," she said, flouncing away. "If Amy comes in and wants to help me with my math homework, I left it on my side of the desk."

"She burns me up," said Lisa after Palmer left the room.

"She just has a difficult temper," Shanon said patiently. "Maybe it's because she has parent problems."

"I should have those kind of problems!" Lisa quipped. "Her mom gives her an unlimited allowance and she has three separate charge accounts! I've had the same allowance since I was ten!"

"Really?" Shanon said, surprised. "Your dad's got so much money, too. I thought I was the only one who had a small allowance. Of course, my dad gives me what he can afford."

"Palmer isn't living up to our deal," Lisa grumbled, back on the subject. "We read her the letters we get from our pen pals, but it's been two weeks since she's showed us anything from John Adams. It just isn't fair!"

"Maybe John's letters are too personal," Shanon giggled, handing Lisa a Styrofoam cup of peppermint tea.

"Yeah, maybe they are," Lisa agreed with a mischievous gleam in her dark eyes. "And to think that Palmer didn't really like John at first! Things must be getting serious between them!"

Shanon grinned. "They must be!"

Lisa glanced at the open door to Palmer and Amy's bedroom. "The door is open," she whispered. "I bet we could find John's letter if we wanted to. Palmer said it was lost in her biology book. Of course that might mean it's lost forever. Palmer never opens any of her books, especially biology."

"We'd better not go snooping through her stuff," said Shanon.

"I guess not," Lisa sighed. She pulled her silky dark hair into a ponytail. "We wouldn't want Amy or Palmer to do that to us."

"No, we wouldn't," Shanon agreed, crossing to the sitting-room bookshelf. She straightened the photograph of the four of them that sat on the middle shelf. It had been taken by her friend, Kate Majors, at the beginning of the school year. Back then, twelve-year-old Shanon, and thirteen-year-olds Amy, Palmer, and Lisa had been just getting to know one another, learning to live together as roommates at the Alma Stephens School for Girls.

Shanon remembered how it had been Palmer who first complained so bitterly about the absence of boys at Alma Stephens. And how Lisa had come up with the idea of advertising for pen pals at the all-boys Ardsley Academy a few miles down the road. The plan had worked, and now each girl had a pen pal who wrote regularly.

Advertising together for their pen pals had brought the four girls much closer. They'd even given themselves a code name, Foxes of the Third Dimension. The Third

Dimension part (after their suite number, 3-D) had drifted away, but the Foxes had stuck. So had The Unknown, the code name their Ardsley pen pals had chosen. Conveniently, the four boys who wrote to them were also suitemates.

Shanon was startled from her thoughts by a sound at the front door of the suite. "Somebody give me a hand, please," Amy Ho called from outside. Shanon met her at the door. In one hand Amy carried her guitar case and in the other she held a long, cylindrical package. Her knapsack full of books was slung over her shoulder and a pair of ice skates hung around her neck.

Amy plopped down on the loveseat. "I was with Brenda. I played the guitar for her at the try-outs. You know, that talent thing they're having during the Winter Festival?"

"Oh, yeah," said Lisa. "I heard about that."

"So you and Brenda are going to do something together?" Shanon asked eagerly. "Sounds great! Maybe I can write a little story about it for *The Ledger*."

"Hold on," said Amy. "I'm not doing anything. I just helped Brenda audition. If she gets into the talent show, she'll have to find another guitarist."

"But you're terrific yourself," said Lisa. "And you sing just as well as Brenda."

"I don't sing," said Amy. "I croak. Don't forget, I'm the one who got thrown out of chorus." She crossed over to the mirror and tugged at her spiky black hair. Amy was Chinese-American, raised mostly in New York City. "Where's Palmer?" she asked.

"In Germaine Richards's room—again," Lisa replied. "But she'll be back. She wants you to help her with her math homework."

Amy chuckled. "Palmer hates numbers." Turning back to her reflection, she added critically, "I need a new haircut. I'm starting to look too conservative."

Lisa giggled. "You? Conservative? Impossible!"

Amy laughed. "I guess you're right! But I still need a hairdresser!"

"You won't find one within twenty-five miles," Shanon assured her, "especially if you want to look modern like you do."

Amy picked up the cylindrical mailing tube she'd brought in and started pacing. "I wish Palmer would get back," she said, "so I could open this." Amy looked at Shanon and Lisa with lively eyes. "It's from Simmie Randolph the Third."

Shanon gasped. "A package from your pen pal!"

"Open it up!" Lisa insisted.

"I have to wait for Palmer," Amy said.

"I don't see Palmer letting you read her letters from John Adams," Lisa pointed out.

Amy shrugged. "Not lately. But she loves it when I get stuff from Simmie."

Just then, Palmer appeared in the doorway, holding a bright green mug. "Hi," she greeted Amy. "Isn't this cool! Germaine made me instant coffee and let me use the mug she got last summer in Paris. She swiped it from a cafe."

"That's just too fabulous," Lisa said sarcastically. "Come in! Amy got something from Simmie."

Palmer blushed and gulped. "From Simmie? You got a package?"

"Yeah, it's a pretty strange shape, too," Amy said, ripping off the tape.

Palmer watched enviously. Of all the Ardsley pen pals,

she was most jealous of Amy's. She had only seen Simmie Randolph III once, just as Amy had. But there wasn't a doubt in her mind that he was the cutest of the Unknowns.

Amy opened the top to the package and peered inside. "Looks like some kind of artwork," she said, pulling out the rolled paper. "It's . . . it's a picture of . . . Simmie."

"A giant blow-up," said Lisa, impressed. "It must be three by four feet!"

"Who cares how big it is?" said Amy. "Look how cute he is!"

"Well, we asked for photographs," breathed Palmer. She couldn't take her eyes off the poster. Simmie looked even better in the blow-up than he had in person. His thick blond hair fell over one eye and his eyes were a brilliant green.

"Do you think he wears green contacts?" Lisa asked.

"No, those are his real eyes," Palmer said dreamily.

"I think you're right," Amy agreed. "Where shall I hang him?" She walked into the bedroom and everyone followed.

"My side of the wall is pretty well covered," she observed. "I guess I'll take down Joan Jett."

"Or you could take down your map of the world," Lisa suggested.

"If it were Mars's picture," piped up Shanon, "I'd hang it right over my bed."

"Here's what we can do," Palmer said suddenly. She crossed to her own side of the bedroom. "My wall is completely empty—see? You can hang it here, Amy."

Amy looked doubtful. "Are you sure? Don't you want to hang something of your own there?"

8

"I can't seem to find the right thing," Palmer said, trying to sound casual. "I don't mind if you use it—really." She grabbed the poster and held it up to the wall space. "See! It's perfect."

Amy smiled. "I'll certainly have a great view when I face your side of the room."

Lisa nodded. "It's a good spot. If the moon is shining at night his face will be lit up," she giggled wickedly.

"That's right," Palmer urged. "There's more sunlight and more moonlight on my side because of the window."

Amy got the tape. "Okay. Let's hang it up. Thanks for letting me use your wall space, Palmer."

"No problem," Palmer said, pleased with herself. "You're always doing things for me. It's about time I returned the favor."

Amy, Lisa, and Shanon went back to the sitting room, but Palmer stayed behind in the bedroom. Plopping onto her bed, she gazed upward at Simmie Randolph III's blown-up image . . . and sighed.

CHAPTER TWO

———◆———

Salve, *Rob Williams, Chief of the Unknowns,*

I am sitting in a chair next to the window in my room. The chair goes with the desk and it is usually on Shanon's side. We have a real neat poster of sunflowers on our wall. I was trying to memorize my Latin vocabulary, but it is too boring. I wish I could go to a movie instead—not to the Assembly Hall but to a real movie theater. I guess they don't have those at Ardsley, either. If they did or if we did, and if one of us were allowed to invite someone over, I would definitely invite you. Or maybe the Foxes would invite all of the Unknowns. What movie would you like to see if we did have a real theater and I could invite you?

I am wearing a pair of purple bike pants, a black and white checked T-shirt, and I've tied the arms of a red sweatshirt around my neck. And I am totally bored with sitting here. That's why I am writing to you.

Oh!! your idea for getting an idea for a story out of the Times *is fantastic. I read a really sad story about a little baby who was left wrapped up in brown paper on this man's doorstep. But the man liked her and took her to a* hospital and the nurses liked her, too. So I guess it had a happy ending. Anyway, I'm going to take the idea of the story for something I have to do for English class. Mr. Griffith will like it. We're supposed to write something on an emotional experience that happened to us. Speaking of emotions, which season do you like best? Summer or winter? I definitely don't like winter.

> Sincerely,
> Lisa McGreevy, Chief of the Foxes

Dear Lisa,

Winter makes me sick too, unless it is snowing. One of my favorite sports is snolf. That is short for snow golf. You steal all your father's golf balls, take them out into the snow and practice your drive. Then, when spring comes, you have lots of little white balls growing up in your lawn when the snow disappears.

I am wearing two T-shirts, jeans, a flannel shirt, a sweater, two pairs of socks and some fur boots. I think I look like the Abominable Snowman.

I would like to see a rerun of E.T. if we went to the movies together. I have seen E.T. twenty-five times, so I wouldn't have to worry about missing anything. Because if I were with you, there's no way I would be watching the movie.

> Yours truly,
> Rob

P.S. Your story idea sounds great. Very emotional. Hope your teacher likes it.

Dear Mars,

It's been a whole week since I've written because there are a lot of quizzes here—one each in French, Latin, math, and biology—and a paper in English. The teachers are trying to get it all in before Thanksgiving. My folks have invited Lisa, Amy, and Palmer to come to my house since we live right in Brighton and they all live far away.

I am sending you a picture of myself. I hope you still want it. I finally got one taken that I think is pretty good. My friend from the newspaper, Kate Majors, took it. Kate is very strange to a lot of people, but she is my friend. Its nice to know somebody who's older, not just in third form like we are. Kate also helped convince the editor of our school paper, The Ledger, to let me write my first article. I was sort of nervous about it because in the story I suggested that Alma sponsor more joint events with Ardsley so the social life would be better. I'm not sure what Miss Pryn the headmistress thought about that.

Simmie sent Amy a poster of himself! By the way, if you have a spare picture of yourself I'd like to have it. It is fun to think of what you look like when I write to you. The one time I saw you at the Halloween Mixer is sort of blurry. I'm glad your pen-holder invention is going well. Write soon.

Your pen pal,
Shanon Davis

P.S. Did John Adams tell you how we talked to each other over the computers?! I was in the newspaper office, he was at your Lit. Mag. office, and we were both online at the same time with this computer Journalism Club. A bunch of people from different schools were having discussions over

12

the computer about our magazines and newspapers and I kept putting out messages to this guy from Ardsley who turned out to be John! What a scream!! I was actually talking to your suitemate. Wouldn't it be great if we all had phones and computers in our rooms? Then we'd have another way of communicating besides letters. Anyway, tell John it was neat. Maybe I'll get him online again sometime.

Dear Pen Pal Shanon Davis,

I got the picture that your friend Kate took of you. Please thank her for me because it is really nice and I put it someplace special. You write such good letters. No wonder you write for the newspaper over there. I gave John Adams your message and he said to say hi. What a coincidence, you being the Alma girl he was chatting with in the computer Journalism Club. Of course he recognized your name as being my pen pal. Maybe I can convince him to let me use the Lit. Mag. computer someday. I'd like to talk to you over the wires too. It would be quicker than a letter. Who knows?—Maybe I'll be able to afford a computer of my own if I keep selling pen holders! It's wild, the guys over here are really ordering the crazy things. I want yours to be special so I'm still working on it.

Again, I am really glad for the pic. I remembered the way you look pretty well. I like really long hair, especially the wavy kind. And your eyes are hazel, right? That means they change colors. I still don't have a pic of myself. Sorry. Maybe you don't really want one, ha ha. Let's just say I'm not the GQ type like Simmie Randolph. I'm more like a young Timothy Hutton—only brasher looking? Figure it

out. I can't. I want to break out of this place. I love
Ard-Barf, but right now it feels kind of like a snowbound
Boy Scout camp. Give me some baseball! But not in
November.

Mars (Alias Arthur Martinez)

Dear Simmie,

Thanks for the poster of yourself!! What a cool idea—a
blow-up! My roommate Palmer Durand (who I think you
met at the Halloween Mixer) and I have hung it up in our
room and it covers one whole wall almost completely.

Have you heard the Tracy Chapman tape? She is a
serious performer. Have you heard about our soccer team?
We are a shoe-in for the finals, and our coach Mrs. Haig is
the best. I'm a forward.

What else am I doing? Oh, yes, I have a gig with this girl
Brenda who is singing for a talent night in this Winter
Festival thing the school has every year. Since this is my
first year here, I don't know what it will be like. Anyway,
I am just practicing with Brenda, playing the guitar for her
until she gets somebody to accompany her for real. She
seems to like practicing with me, and I do enjoy playing, so
I don't mind—for a while, anyway. I am also onto a new
level in math. They keep moving me to different classes.
My suitemate Lisa thinks I am a genius. But I just like
playing with decimals.

Signing off,
Amy HO-HO-HO
(Just getting ready for the holidays)

P.S. By the way, where did you get that picture of yourself
blown up? I'd like to do the same thing with a picture of

the Foxes of the Third Dimension someone took at the beginning of the year.

P.P.S. I don't know if I already told you this, but I've been writing to an old school friend of mine—Evon—from Australia, and she's just invited me to Sydney for Christmas vacation! Too bad my parents just decided that for once we're actually going to spend the holidays all together. Oh well . . . maybe next year.

Dear Amy,

Like I always said, you are amuzing. "Ho-Ho-Ho" is pretty funny. But what is a decimal? Just kidding! I'm not that stupid, though math is not exactly my favorite subgect.

Too bad you won't be going to Australia for Christmas. Rob says that they have summer there when it's winter here. Sounds great to me. I find it really cold here. I am used to being in Florida at this time of year or at least the Bahamas. My folks have a house there and I will probably fly down for Thanksgiving. I have not heard of Tracy Chapman yet. I'm glad you and your roomate Palmer Durand apreciate the blow-up of me. I think it came out good too. That is a new jacket. I will send you the adress of the place to order the poster. I would like to see that blow-up of the Foxes of the Third Dimenssion when it arives myself. Having a picture of all four of you girls in our suite would be great! Say hello to Palmer and tell her I'm glad she likes my picture.

Yours very truly,
Simmie Randolph III
(Just call me Three or Trois—I learned that in French)

15

Dear Palmer,

My work at the Lit. Mag. here is going really fine. I was shocked of course when I got taken on. They didn't like the TORTURED poem, but they think I have promise. I am working on something new about how I feel in winter. It's called "Cabin Fever." It's too early to show it to you yet. Hey, you never said anything about the last letter I wrote. In fact, you haven't written in a while. Is something the matter? Are you too busy studying? I guess Shanon Davis told you that we had a "conference" so to speak over the computer when we were both online with this new thing the Lit. Mag. has subscribed to called the Journalism Club. The Club is pretty informative, but when I got Shanon online I kind of wished it was you instead. And that we weren't sending messages about just news stories.

I want to know how come you're not writing to me, Palmer. Please explain. I also want to know more about you. I still remember how you looked at the Halloween Mixer. Your She-Ra was sensational. And that picture you sent of yourself in the party dress is nice too. But your personality remains a puzzle. Who are you? She-Ra the sensational or a junior debutante? Or maybe you're a combination—maybe you're deb-sational! Write soon or something.

> *Your pen pal,*
> *John Adams*

Palmer read John's letter over again and thought back to their meeting at the Halloween Mixer. All she could remember was that he was tall and had red hair and looked serious. He was cute but not as cute as Simmie Randolph.

16

"Deb-sational?" she muttered in frustration. What was John Adams talking about? And what was he doing asking about her personality? How was she supposed to write something on such a difficult subject? Writing to John was worse than doing homework.

Palmer scrunched down at her desk and tore a sheet of paper from her notebook. Idly, she tapped the lined page with the top of her pen. Her mind was as blank as the paper. Finally, she began to write. . . .

Dear John,
I have nothing to say.

Signed,
Palmer Durand

CHAPTER THREE

"So what are your suitemates like?" Germaine asked slyly. "I mean really like?"

"Odd," Palmer said, providing the answer she knew Germaine was after. "They're really into school activities, and all."

"Gruesome," Germaine said with a shudder, waving her hand limply. Palmer couldn't help noticing the elegance of her friend's well-cared-for nails. Germaine, who was in fourth form, paid one of the third-formers to manicure them on a regular basis.

"I really like your hair that way," Palmer said, sipping a cup of Germaine's instant coffee. Germaine's long auburn hair was brushed back on one side, while the other part hung in the front, almost completely covering one eye.

"Thanks," Germaine said smugly. "Your friend Shanon could use a haircut."

"She has no sense of style," agreed Palmer.

"And that Lisa looks like a beanpole," Germaine giggled.

18

Palmer felt a twinge. She wanted Germaine to know that she was much more sophisticated and worldly than her suitemates, but she felt disloyal making fun of them. "She is kind of tall, it's true," Palmer said matter-of-factly.

Germaine curled her feet up. She was wearing patent leather heels, a silk dress, and dark red lipstick. Palmer made a note of the dress—she'd like to find one just like it.

Germaine took a lipstick out of her pocket and tossed the tube to Palmer. Even though makeup was against the dress code at Alma, it was Saturday afternoon and there wasn't much chance of getting caught.

"Amy Ho's into rock 'n' roll, huh?" Germaine went on. "How dumb. And she's so punk-looking."

"Yeah, she's into that." Palmer shrugged. "How's your boyfriend?" she asked, to change the subject.

"Which one?" answered Germaine, with a crooked smile.

Palmer gasped. "You mean you've got more than one, now?"

"Try three," said Germaine.

Palmer's mouth dropped open. "You're incredible, Germaine. How do you do it?"

"Easy," Germaine answered. "At the last Ardsley Mixer I met two guys and both of them were crazy about me. So now I'm going steady with both of them. And then, there's my old boyfriend from elementary school."

"He still likes you?" said Palmer.

Germaine smiled broadly. "What can I say?"

Palmer sighed. "I sure could take some lessons from you."

"I thought you were all fixed up with your pen pal," said

19

Germaine. "Aren't you writing to that guy ... John Adams?"

"I don't like John," Palmer said stubbornly.

"What's wrong?" Germaine strolled across the room to put on some perfume. "Isn't he cute enough?"

"That's not it," Palmer explained. "I just don't understand him. You know what he likes to do? ... Write poetry!"

Germaine closed her eyes. "Bor-ing."

Palmer nodded in agreement.

"I hear that Amy's a real dweeb," Germaine said, turning the conversation back to the Foxes.

"She's a math genius," Palmer grunted. "And Shanon Davis is a literary type. She's on scholarship and has—get this—already written an article for *The Ledger*. They usually don't even let third-formers *on* the newspaper."

"Yeah, she's the one who wrote that ridiculous article about having more extracurricular activities," Germaine said jealously.

Palmer didn't say anything. Although she was jealous of Shanon, too, she knew in her heart that the article had been quite good.

"Anyway," Palmer picked up, "I haven't been writing to John much these days. Only none of the other girls knows about it. I haven't made up my mind what I'm going to do about John."

Germaine lifted an eyebrow. "John's not the one on the poster over your bed, huh?"

Palmer sighed. "No, that's Simmie. But he's Amy's pen pal."

"Too bad," said Germaine. "It's a shame that a cute boy

like Simmie is wasted on an oddball like Amy Ho. I think you and he would make an adorable couple."

Palmer blushed. She had daydreamed a thousand times about Simmie Randolph III. There was no boy in the world who looked as good as he did. If Alma was a co-ed school and they had classes together she would be able to bump into him. Then he might just naturally come to like her better than he liked Amy. After all, she and Simmie had a lot more in common. They were both blond and came from Florida. But daydreaming that she and Simmie went to school together wasn't going to make it happen.

Palmer smoothed out her soft wool skirt. Both the skirt and her cashmere sweater were the same color blue as her eyes. "Well, I'm stuck with John," she muttered. "I guess I'll just have to make the best of it."

"You really are young for your age," Germaine sighed.

"Some people think I'm fourteen," boasted Palmer. "Nobody ever said I looked young before."

"I'm not talking about looks," Germaine told her. "It's a question of attitude. Haven't you ever heard the rule that all is fair when it comes to boyfriends?"

Palmer blushed. "I don't think so."

"Believe me," Germaine said knowingly, "it's true." She settled back onto her bed and leafed through some mail-order catalogues. "How do you think I got three boyfriends?"

Palmer swallowed and strolled over to Germaine's mirror. She didn't like the way this conversation was going. Was Germaine suggesting that she try to steal Simmie from Amy? As much as she melted over Simmie, she couldn't do that to Amy. . . . Could she?

21

"That color looks good on you," Germaine said approvingly. "Come on, let's order some more clothes from these catalogues. Which of these outfits do you think Simmie Randolph the Third would like to see you wear?"

On that same Saturday afternoon, Amy was busy practicing for Talent Night with her friend Brenda. The two girls were sitting on the edge of Amy's bed.

"Let's take that part of the song from the break again," Amy said. "Something just isn't right."

"Okay," said Brenda, clearing her throat loudly.

"What are you doing that with your voice for?" Amy asked.

"Trying to make it sound hoarse," Brenda answered. "I'm afraid I sound too soprano-ish."

Amy chuckled. "With a great voice like yours I wouldn't complain."

"But I sound like a folk singer," Brenda argued.

"Relax," said Amy. "You'll be terrific. Did you get somebody to play for you the night of the talent show?"

"Not exactly," Brenda said nervously. She stared across the room and her eye fell on Palmer's bed. It was loaded with sweaters. "Whose stuff is that?"

"Palmer's," Amy replied.

"Wow," murmured Brenda. "It looks brand new. What's she going to do with all those?"

Amy shrugged. "Wear them, I guess. Palmer likes clothes."

Brenda giggled. "So I've heard. Dolores Countee called Palmer a giant Barbie doll because she has such a big wardrobe."

22

"That's not funny," Amy snapped. "Palmer's my room-mate."

Brenda blushed. "Sorry. I wasn't the one who said it."

"Sorry I jumped on you," said Amy. "But the four of us in the suite are kind of tight."

Brenda smiled. "Yeah I know . . . the Foxes. I see you eating together all the time. It's nice that you're so loyal to Palmer Durand, but if I were you—"

Amy picked up her guitar. "Let's practice."

She played the intro to the Springsteen song Brenda had chosen to sing. Amy secretly thought that the number wasn't quite right for her. But she didn't want to say anything to make Brenda any more nervous than she was already.

Brenda stopped abruptly. "I just can't do this song."

"Well . . . maybe it's not the right choice," Amy suggested gently.

Brenda looked alarmed. "You mean after all this work, you think I should change songs?"

"I didn't say that," Amy cut in quickly. "But you said so yourself."

Brenda sighed. "The trouble is, I can't think of anything better. Maybe I should just forget about Talent Night."

"You auditioned and got the spot, though," Amy protested. "I know what. . . ." She strummed a few bars of a melody.

"What's that?" asked Brenda, perking up.

"Just something I've been fooling around with," said Amy, continuing to play. "It might go well with your kind of voice."

"It's a great melody," Brenda said, getting excited. "How do the words go?"

"That's the problem," Amy said, stopping abruptly. "All I've got is a few lines."

"What's the song supposed to be about?" Brenda asked.

"It's about a feeling you get in winter," Amy explained. "Sort of like you want to jump out of your whole body."

"Like cabin fever?" said Brenda.

Amy smiled. "That's what I'm talking about." She picked up the guitar again and strummed loudly. "That's what I'm talking about!" she bellowed in a low, strong voice. "That's what I'm talking about!"

"Great!" said Brenda. "You sound fantastic."

"I sound awful," Amy said bluntly. "But I do think the song has potential."

Brenda's eyes lit up. "Wouldn't it be incredible to do an original song for Talent Night?"

"Uh-uh," said Amy, shaking her head. "It's not ready yet."

"But you've got a few weeks," Brenda argued. "That melody is so great for my voice. I'd really like to try it."

Amy felt a rush of excitement. "Maybe I could work on it," she said, strumming again, only this time more softly.

"Just think cabin fever," Brenda urged, "and maybe more words will come to you."

CHAPTER FOUR

"What a horrible day!" said Amy, trotting across the quadrangle.

"I'm freezing," muttered Palmer through her muffler.

"Talk about freezing!" exclaimed Lisa. "I think my bangs are turning into icicles."

"They are!" gasped Shanon. "I told you to dry your hair when you got out of the shower!"

The Foxes crunched across the icy grass toward Booth Hall for Miss Pryn's weekly "Four o'Clock." There had been nothing but cold rain and sleet all week. What was visible of the sun was already setting.

"This is the worst weather I've ever seen," Palmer complained, shivering. "This dampness is ruining my good rabbit coat!" She pulled her fur hat down farther; as she walked, her high-heeled boots kept sinking.

"Yes, I wish it would hurry up and snow again," Shanon agreed. "It looks so pretty when everything's covered up."

Amy picked up speed. "Let's just get there!" she suggested cheerfully. The wind tore at her open black peacoat.

Underneath she had a big turtleneck and a down vest. Palmer struggled to keep up with her, while Shanon and Lisa brought up the rear.

"I wonder what Miss Pryn's going to talk about this week," Lisa said. "Maybe those new courses you suggested in your news article. Wouldn't that be funny?"

"Miss Pryn wouldn't talk about my article at a Four o'Clock," said Shanon shyly.

When they reached Booth Hall, they hung up their coats and headed straight for the lecture hall. The large room was buzzing as they walked in. Four o'Clocks were a big event, especially because of the tea in the library that was always held afterwards. Up front near the podium was the imposing-looking headmistress Miss Pryn. And next to the stage, talking to Brenda and a group of other girls, stood the youngest faculty member, Maggie Grayson. Miss Grayson taught French and was also the Fox Hall faculty advisor. "Doesn't she look pretty!" whispered Lisa. "She's wearing her lavender dress!"

"Where's Mr. Griffith?" Shanon whispered back.

"There he is." Amy gestured toward their tall, good-looking English teacher standing in the aisle just a few yards away. Every girl in the school had a crush on him. And everyone was absolutely positive that he liked Miss Grayson. The girls watched as Mr. Griffith peered across the crowded room. When he spotted Miss Grayson down front, he made a beeline in her direction.

"There he goes," giggled Palmer.

"What do you want to bet they get engaged before the end of the year," said Lisa.

Miss Pryn rapped on the podium and the room quieted

down. Miss Grayson and Mr. Griffith took seats in the front together. The Foxes slid into the back row. Palmer glanced around for Germaine but couldn't find her.

"Winter is upon us," Miss Pryn began. Her voice was so strong that she never needed a microphone. "It can be a gloomy season with its late dawns and early sunsets or it can be a season full of fun! Here at Alma Stephens, we try to make it the latter."

Palmer groaned beneath her breath. "Let's get to the tea scones."

"Each year," Miss Pryn continued, "we have two days of winter sports and a talent night. We call it the Winter Festival."

A murmur of excitement ran through the room.

"I wonder what it's like," said Lisa.

Amy grinned. "I bet it'll be fun."

"This year," Miss Pryn went on, "we have a surprise development. Due to various requests for improvement in the social life here, some of which were pointed out in an article in *The Ledger*—"

Lisa elbowed Shanon. "She's talking about your article," she gasped excitedly.

Miss Pryn eyed the gathering. "We have decided to sponsor the Winter Festival in conjunction with Ardsley Academy."

The hall was filled with buzzing again as the girls broke out into excited conversations.

"Did you hear that?" said Lisa. "Ardsley's coming. We'll get to see our pen pals."

"Great!" cried Amy.

Shanon's hands flew to her face. "I'll get to see Mars!"

27

Palmer thought about John Adams. "Whoopee," she mouthed sarcastically.

Miss Pryn put up her hands to hush the crowd. "The details of the Festival will be made available and posted," she told them. "There will be ice-skating, tobogganing, snow sculpture, cross-country ski races, and an exhibition of downhill, among other things, for boys *and* girls. The Ardsley boys will be bused in on the morning of each day and return to their school in the evening. And an invitation has been extended to them to stay for Saturday's Talent Night. I hope you will enjoy the festivities."

The room burst into applause and Miss Pryn smiled. "Of course, I'm sure I don't have to remind you to comport yourselves with the dignity Alma Stephens girls are known for. On no account will boys be allowed in the dormitories except in the areas of the common rooms, and that only during certain hours. Details will be posted. Now, let's have our tea."

The murmur of conversations rose to a roar as the girls filed out of the room. "I can't believe this is happening," said Lisa. "I'm going to faint. To think I'll be with Rob for two whole days! He'll even be able to come into the dorm!"

"Only in the common room," Shanon warned her. "I just hope I can remember what Mars looks like."

"I *know* what John looks like," said Palmer dully.

"I guess the next step is to write to them and make sure they're coming," said Amy. "I wonder if Simmie is any kind of ice skater. That's what I'm up for."

As the girls crowded down the hall toward the library common room, Palmer felt a hand on her shoulder. It was Germaine.

"Where were you?" Palmer asked her.

"I always skip those things," Germaine said. "I come to the last part for the tea scones."

"Good idea."

"I heard about the Festival, though. Aren't you excited about having the boys come?"

"Why should I be?" Palmer pouted. "I can just see myself spending two days listening to John Adams's poetry."

"Who says you have to spend your time with *John?*" Germaine said slyly.

"He's the only boy I know from Ardsley," said Palmer.

"He's not the *only* boy you know," said Germaine.

"What do you mean?" asked Palmer.

"Have you forgotten S.R. the Third?" Germaine giggled.

Palmer was puzzled for a moment, but then she got it. "Oh, you mean Simmie!"

"Exactly," said Germaine as she flounced into the library. "Remember my motto—when it comes to boys, there's no such thing as unfair."

CHAPTER FIVE

———◆———

"Where did you learn to give haircuts like this?" asked Amy. She was sitting in a chair in the middle of the sitting-room floor with a sheet around her shoulders.

"I used to cut our poodle at home," explained Lisa.

Amy jerked her head. "Your poodle? Don't tell me I'm going to have a dog cut!"

Lisa giggled. "Relax. Reggie let me cut his hair a couple of times last summer. Everyone said it looked good. Anyway, I'm just following the line of your original haircut."

"I hope I'm doing the right thing," Amy said, shutting her eyes. "The last thing in the world I want is to look like a poodle when I see Simmie."

"This is a really good first paragraph, Lisa!" Shanon said. She was at the desk reading Lisa's English paper. "It's very emotional-sounding."

"Thanks," Lisa said, keeping her eyes on the scissors. "I hope Mr. Griffith likes it. He hasn't been too thrilled with my other papers. Now, all I have to do is finish it."

"Did all of this really happen to you?" Shanon asked.

"Well . . ." Lisa hemmed. "Actually, Rob gave me the idea. It's not his idea, but . . . it's a long story."

Just then Palmer rushed into the room. "There you are!" Amy exclaimed. "We've been wondering what happened to you. We have to write our invitation to The Unknown for the Festival."

Palmer shrugged. "How can you write to The Unknown when you're getting your hair cut?"

"She wants to look good for Simmie," Lisa bubbled. "The Winter Festival is only five weeks away!"

"Deb-sational," Palmer muttered. "By that time she'll need another one."

"What did you say?" asked Shanon.

"Deb-sational," Palmer replied in a monotone. "It's just a word John wrote in a letter."

"Guess you can't wait to see John," Shanon said enthusiastically.

"You bet!" Palmer said, smiling archly. "By the way," she asked, trying to appear casual, "where's that folder that we had on The Unknown?"

"The one with the questionnaires?" said Shanon. "It's on the bottom of the bookshelf stuck between my thesaurus and Lisa's horse book.

Palmer rolled her eyes. "Boy are you organized." She sauntered over to the bookshelf.

Amy stood up and shook out the sheet. "No kidding, this haircut is okay," she said, examining herself in the mirror.

"Here, spike it," Lisa suggested, handing her a can of mousse.

Amy foamed up her hair. "This is great, Lisa, honest. You could start a business."

"Like that girl upstairs who does manicures," Shanon giggled.

Amy and Lisa burst out laughing.

"I wouldn't go that far," said Lisa.

"Can you believe anyone our age would go in for manicures!" said Amy. "I wonder who her customers are."

"Germaine's one of them," Palmer said stiffly. "She wants her hands to be professional-looking and I don't blame her."

Amy hooted. "Maybe I should get a manicure for when I play the guitar! I sure wouldn't want my hands to look unprofessional."

There was a tense silence in the room. Lisa, Amy, and Shanon eyed one another. It was obvious that Palmer was not amused.

"Did you find John's old questionnaire?" Shanon asked, changing the subject.

Palmer blushed. "What?" She held The Unknown's folder to her chest.

"You really like John, don't you?" said Lisa.

"I . . . I guess," Palmer stammered.

Amy brushed her clothes off. "Remember how much trouble we had getting The Unknowns to complete those questionnaires?"

"Yeah, they weren't too cooperative," said Lisa.

Shanon laughed softly. "And then when we sent them a second one . . ."

"Well, I guess we all know them pretty well by now,"

said Amy brightly. "After all, we've been writing for over two months. Simmie's letters are pretty short, but I still think he's neat."

Palmer tucked the folder under her arm and moved toward her bedroom.

"Where are you going?" said Lisa. "Don't you want to help write the invitation? We want to make sure the guys come to the Winter Festival."

"I'm sure that whatever you three decide to write will be okay," Palmer replied.

"I've got some silver paper," Lisa said. "Maybe we can make the invitation out of that. And I guess we should include a copy of the schedule."

"That's right," agreed Shanon. "Suppose Mars signs up for tobogganing at the same time I'm doing cross-country skiing? Then we'd miss each other!"

"Ummm," Lisa grunted. "Besides the invitation, we should probably write individually to make sure we can coordinate things."

"I'm going to sign up for ice-skating," said Amy. "I hope that Simmie will like that."

"I sure hope I remember what Mars looks like," Shanon murmured.

"I know what you mean," said Lisa. "When I try to think of Rob's face, all I can see is his curly hair."

Palmer slipped out of the room. She could hardly wait to look at the questionnaires in The Unknown's folder. She leafed past John's two questionnaires carelessly. When she came to the ones with Simmie's name on the top, she crept over to the door and closed it. Then, settling down on her bed, she began to read.

33

QUESTIONNAIRE
FROM FOXES OF THE THIRD DIMENSION
TO THE UNKNOWN

NAME: Simmie Randolph III

AGE: 14

Please answer these questions.

If you were a flower or plant, what would you be?

ROSE

If you were a country, what would you be?

PALM BEACH, FLORIDA

If you were a musical instrument, what would you be?

NOTHING

If you were an animal, what would you be?

LION, KING OF THE JUNGLE

If you were an ice cream cone, what flavor would you be?

CHOCOLATE SWIRL

If you were a car, what car would you be?

RED JAGUAR, WHICH I'M GETTING IN 2 YRS.

If you were a book, what book would you be?

DON'T KNOW

If you were a record, what record would you be?

DON'T KNOW

If you were a color, what color would you be?

YELLOW

If you were an insect, what insect would you be?

SCORPION

Would you be an insect at all?

SCORPION

NAME: Simmie Randolph III

Please write down your hobbies:

SKIING, TENNIS, SKIING

Please write down your favorite subjects in school:

NONE

Please write down your favorite sports:

SKIING AND TENNIS

Please write down your favorite place:

THE BEACH

Please write down what you like most to eat.

LOBSTER, STEAK, CHOCOLATE CAKE

Please write down an interesting dream:

I AM DRIVING MY RED JAGUAR, WHICH

I WILL SOON OWN AT AGE 16 AS

IT HAS BEEN PROMISED TO ME BY

MY FATHER. AND I AM COMING

TO A CLIFF. BUT WINGS GROW

FROM THE TIRES AND I START

TO FLY.

CHAPTER SIX

EXTRA, EXTRA!
READ ALL ABOUT IT!
WINTER FESTIVAL AT ALMA!
THE FOXES OF THE THIRD DIMEN-
SION, Lisa Ann McGreevy, Amy Ho, Sha-
non Marlene Davis, and Palmer Stuyvesant
Durand, cordially invite THE ARD-BARF
UNKNOWNS to the Winter Festival Sat-
urday and Sunday (all day!! and Saturday
evening) December 10 and 11 at Alma
Stephens Prison for Girls! Respondez Si
Vous Plait! Please indicate what activities
you would like to do.

TOBOGGANING
CROSS-COUNTRY SKIING
SNOW SCULPTURE
CURLING
SLEDDING
DOWNHILL SKI EXHIBITION
FIGURE- OR SPEED-SKATING

Dear Rob,

What does the Abominable Snowman really look like? Don't tell me it looks like you! No matter how many layers you are wearing. I remember that you do look like a human.

I love snow sculpture, and there is a competition for the best one. You do the sculpture on Saturday and it's judged on Sunday morning. Also there is the Talent Night, which I hope you'll want to come to. My suitemate Amy is helping out somebody who is singing in it. WRIGHT RITE AWAY!!!

Lisa

Dear Mars,

I guess you know about the Winter Festival. We are really excited about it. What kinds of winter sports do you like? I am putting in a list of activities. I'm not too good at downhill, but I like cross-country skiing. Let me know what you'd like to do. In any case, I hope you'll come. I think it's going to be fun. Please write and let me know.

Shanon

P.S. Maybe you can advertise your pen holders in The Ledger.

Dear John,

I am sure it will be all right if you come to the Festival at Alma, but I'm not sure I should be the one to invite you. To tell the truth, there is another person who might take up a lot of my time. And anyway, I don't like winter sports. Hope this does not hurt your feelings. I am sure you

37

are a very nice person, though I don't really know you.
Good luck with your poetry. I'm sure it is very good.

> Yours truly,
> Palmer Stuyvesant Durand

Dear Simmie,

This Winter Festival thing is going to be incredible! You absolutely MUST COME! MUST! Actually, I have decided that I am letting this girl Brenda sing a song I wrote myself for Talent Night. Naturally, I am feeling shaky about this, especially since I'm having trouble with the lyrics. But I'd really like for my pen pal to be there. As for daytime activities, how about ice-skating? There is figure-skating or a speed race which, if I'm feeling brave, I might be interested in. But let me know what you want to do and I'm sure we can do two things. Wish me luck on the lyrics to my song!

Thanks for the address for the poster blow-up. I'm sending away for one. Palmer, Amy, and Lisa will love it. See you in a few weeks.

> Sincerely,
> Amy

P.S. Have a Happy Thanksgiving!

Dear Simmie,

You don't know me, but I know you. And I would like to meet you. I cannot tell you who I am right now, but let's say that my favorite color is yellow and skiing is my absolutely favorite sport in the world next to tennis. I am an Alma girl who is thirteen years old and I have been in *the newspaper in Palm Beach Florida in "Pretty Young Faces" in the Society section. If you would like to meet me in person, I will be at the Winter Festival. I will let you know who I am then, but only if you don't have a date with someone.*

Yours truly,
A Secret Admirer, "P"

As Palmer folded the letter and quickly put it in the envelope, she was surprised to feel a guilty pang of conscience. But she decided to ignore it. Amy wouldn't care that much, she told herself. Jumping up from the desk, she headed off to show Germaine her letter to Simmie. Germaine would definitely approve.

CHAPTER SEVEN

———⬦———

"Run in place! Lift those knees! Come on! Don't be slugs!"
Coach Haig shouted. "This Thursday we're going to show
St. Ann's what we're made of!"

It was cold out on the field, but Amy was boiling in her
sweatpants. Mrs. Haig was tough. Though the soccer
coach was in her seventies, there was no talk at Alma of
retiring her. Every spring she still went to Boston to run in
the Marathon.

"Go, Ho!" the coach bellowed. "Keep it up!" She blew
her whistle, and the team fell in for give-and-go.

Amy threw herself into it. She loved soccer practice. It
was the one time during the day when she didn't feel
restless—the one sure cure for cabin fever.

Her body buzzed as she sprinted back and forth down
the field. She loved soccer almost as much as she loved
music. *Talking about a head disease,* the words jangled in
her brain, *a breakout in the snow . . . my mind's on fire . . .
talking about . . .* She kicked the ball hard. *Cabin fever!* she
thought, sprinting back down the field. *Cabin fever . . .*

No. Those words were no good. But she had to come up with some lyrics to her song—and soon.

"Fall out!" commanded Mrs. Haig. "Good work!" Winded, Amy jogged inside to the locker room.

"We're definitely ready for that match with St. Ann's," Dolores Countee said, bumping by her. Dolores was just about everything at Alma—editor of *The Ledger,* head of the Social Committee, and also one of the soccer team's forwards. Everybody else seemed to think Dolores was the greatest, but Amy didn't like her much—especially after hearing Dolores's "Barbie doll" putdown of Palmer.

"Shanon told me you're writing a song for Brenda Smith to sing at Talent Night," Dolores chattered. Peeling off her sweats, she twisted her long red hair into a bun.

Amy got ready for her shower. "That's the plan."

Dolores smiled broadly. "Well, I think it's remarkable. Brenda's got a lovely voice, and I'm sure you're very talented, too."

Amy grabbed a towel. "Thanks!" she called over her shoulder.

"I can't wait to hear it!" Dolores sang after her. "And aren't you lucky to have such a big audience! Isn't it incredible that Ardsley—"

Amy slammed into one of the individual stalls and turned on the water. All this talk about the song was making her nervous. The fact was, it just wasn't right yet. The melody was perfect, and she'd found a key that was right for Brenda. But the words just didn't say what she wanted them to.

She stuck her head under the shower and hummed in a throaty voice. "Want to go outside and play, but teacher

41

tells me to stay . . . don't she know I got this sickness . . .

"It's sick all right!" she muttered, coming out and wrapping up in a towel. "It's going to be sick if I don't get this song right."

"Talking to yourself?" Dolores said, smiling again.

"Sorry," Amy muttered. The chilly air of the locker room hit her and she held her towel closer. "I'm just thinking about something. . . ." She got her clothes out of her locker and moved away from Dolores.

It was people like Dolores Countee and Germaine Richards she was worried about, upperclassmen who might judge her song harshly. They'd all be in the audience. The whole school would be. And now that the boys from Ardsley had been invited, Simmie'd be there too—along with the other Unknowns.

Suddenly Amy thought having her song in Talent Night wasn't such a good idea after all. Think how embarrassed Brenda would be if nobody clapped for her. As it was, Brenda was having trouble getting an accompanist. And no way was Amy going to get up there on the stage! Her performing days were over and done with, after she'd gotten kicked out of Chorus . . .

Chorus had been a mistake in the first place, she thought. First the conductor had gotten mad at her for tapping her feet. And then he said she bobbed her head too much, that she took away from the picture. But how could she make herself *not* keep time to the music? And then on top of that, she'd been required to read music, something she'd always avoided.

Turning on the overhead dryer, she fluffed out her hair. Then she put on her Walkman and finished dressing. Joan

42

Jett's music made her feel better. *That's the kind of music I want to write,* Amy thought, *only it won't be Joan Jett or Tracy Chapman talking, it'll be me.* Still, *somebody else* would be performing her music, she admitted to herself. Amy knew that being a performer of any kind was nothing but a dream for her—a dream that never would come true. How could it? She couldn't sing. Besides, her father would never let her. Her father hated rock 'n' roll and thought she should be a scientist.

When Amy took off her Walkman, Dolores was at her elbow. "If I don't get a chance to talk with you before Talent Night," Dolores chirped, "good luck! It must be wonderful to be an artist! Of course, I'm an artist myself. I do a bit of singing. Did you know that?"

"I didn't," Amy said dully.

"And Brenda Smith is so incredibly excited!" Dolores continued. "Brenda says singing your original song in Talent Night is the most important thing that's ever happened to her!"

Amy swallowed. "Brenda said that?"

Dolores nodded.

Well that's it, Amy thought. She couldn't back out now. Not if it was that important to Brenda. Grabbing her coat and earphones, she ran out of the gym ahead of Dolores, her brain already wrestling with new lyrics. *Oh it's mad, winter's the fad, but my temperature's way above normal. . . .*

43

CHAPTER EIGHT

". . . My heart is warm with the friends I make, And better friends I'll not be knowing." Mr. Griffith's mellow voice filled the classroom. "Yet there isn't a train I wouldn't take no matter where it's going. . . ." Shanon stared at the teacher, mesmerized, while Lisa doodled absently in her notebook. Amy squirmed in her seat and Palmer stared out the window.

"What do you think Edna St. Vincent Millay was saying in that stanza?" Mr. Griffith asked the class, putting down his poetry book. "Amy?"

"I think she was restless," Amy answered. "She wanted to keep exploring things even though she liked her friends."

"Good analysis," smiled Mr. Griffith. He peered over Lisa's notebook. "Can you relate to those feelings, Miss McGreevy?"

Lisa blushed and covered the page she'd been scribbling on. She'd been writing *Rob Williams*, *Robert Williams*, and *Robbie Williams*, surrounded by hearts, over and over. "Well, Lisa?" said Mr. Griffith.

"I can relate to them, I guess," Lisa answered, still flustered. "I can't wait to go home for the holidays."

"Only you won't be on a train," quipped Palmer. "You'll be on an airplane." The class broke up into giggles.

"And what do *you* think of the poem I just read, Miss Durand?" Mr. Griffith asked, strolling over to the side of the room where Palmer was sitting.

"I'm . . . not certain," Palmer said, smiling cutely. "I have to give it time to sink in."

"You *were* to have reviewed the material before class," he reminded her.

"Sorry, Mr. Griffith," she drawled sweetly. "It just . . . uh, takes me a while to get this stuff." Actually, she hadn't bothered to read the assignment, and when Mr. Griffith had been reading the poem, the only part she'd heard was about the train. She'd had her mind on other things, like Simmie Randolph.

"Class dismissed," Mr. Griffith sighed, looking at the clock. Palmer and Amy both bolted. Shanon headed for Mr. Griffith, while Lisa gathered her notebooks.

"I really loved that poem," Shanon said at Mr. Griffith's elbow. "I really love Edna St. Vincent Millay." She struggled to speak. "You're . . . I mean, she's so . . . incredible." She took a breath and joined Lisa.

"I'm glad you liked the assignment," Mr. Griffith said cheerfully. "Oh, Lisa . . ."

Lisa was standing at the door with her bookbag, waiting for Shanon. "Yes, Mr. Griffith?"

"I was very impressed by your composition," Mr. Griffith said warmly. "You painted the details so realistically. Outstanding improvement. If you don't mind, I'd like to show it around the department."

"Sure . . . thanks," Lisa said, flushing with pleasure.

"You see! I told you your paper was good," Shanon

said, once they were outside the classroom. Amy was pacing the hallway. "Mr. Griffith thought Lisa's story was good," Shanon told Amy.

"Congrats," said Amy. "He didn't say much about mine. I wrote about my experience the first time I heard Paul Simon sing in person."

"I wrote about how emotional I was when I got my scholarship to Alma," said Shanon.

"Let's go to the snack bar!" Lisa suggested. "Gammy sent me twenty dollars this week. I'll treat you to sodas! But first let's go check our mailboxes! Where's Palmer—in the bathroom?"

"I hope she's not putting on makeup again," Shanon sighed. "She's just asking to get into trouble."

"Palmer's not in the bathroom," Amy said, sounding dejected. "She's . . . I guess she's not going to have lunch with us today."

"But we always have lunch together," Shanon protested. "Don't tell me she's on a diet?"

"No, she said she had somewhere else to go," Amy continued. "She didn't tell me where."

"Probably somewhere with Germaine," Lisa muttered. "Anybody would think that Germaine Richards lives with Palmer and not us."

"Maybe she's not with Germaine," Shanon said. "Maybe Palmer went to the French lab. She hasn't been doing too well in that subject."

"She hasn't been doing great in anything," Amy noted, looking worried. "I used to try to help her with her math, but now she doesn't ask me anymore."

"Well, it's her loss if she doesn't want to sit with the Foxes," declared Lisa.

46

There were letters in all three of their mailboxes. Lisa had two envelopes—one from her grandmother and one with "R. W., Kirby Hall" on the return address.

"It's from Rob," she said breathlessly.

"I got one too," sighed Shanon. "It's from Mars. I can tell by his handwriting."

Amy pulled out an envelope.

"Is it from Simmie?" Lisa asked excitedly.

"No, it's from Australia," Amy replied, noticing the colorful stamps. "It must be from my friend Evon." She shoved her hand into the mailbox a second time. "Guess that's it for today," she said, trying to cover her disappointment.

Inside the snack bar, they lodged themselves at their favorite table, the one in the middle of the room near all the ketchup, and Lisa went up front to order their burgers.

Amy looked around casually to see who else was in the snack bar. Her eyes went wide when she saw Palmer sitting with Germaine in a corner. "Wow, look!" she whispered. "Palmer was coming here all along, only it was to meet Germaine."

"Maybe she had something important to discuss with her," Shanon said gently.

Kate Majors stopped by, carrying a load of books. She was wearing a long woolen hat that made her look kind of elfish, and her glasses were slipping.

"Dolores approved your story idea for the Winter Festival," she told Shanon.

"You mean I can write something about the acts at Talent Night?" Shanon asked excitedly.

"Not only that," Kate said, "but we'd like you to throw

47

in some coverage of a few sporting events—like the downhill competition."

Shanon gulped. "Wow! I thought *you* guys were going to cover that."

"We are," Kate informed her. "But Dolores wants a story from a third-former's perspective. It's your first time at the Winter Festival. You'll see it differently from the way we do."

"In—incredible!" Shanon stuttered, hardly able to believe her luck. She had started out as a humble gofer at *The Ledger* and now she was doing big stories.

Lisa bounded back over to the table. "Hi, Kate," she said, barely looking at the older girl. "How's it going?" She pulled the letter from Rob out of her bookbag. "Get yours out," she whispered to Shanon.

Kate lifted an eyebrow. "Still writing to your pen pals?"

"You bet," boasted Lisa. "Our pen pal exchange has really worked out. Remember what a bad idea you thought it was when we first put the advertisement in at Ardsley?"

"Oh, I don't think it's a bad idea now!" Kate said hastily. "I've even been writ—" She stopped abruptly and looked down at the floor. "I mean . . . see you later."

"Bye, Kate," Shanon said. "And thank you!"

"I thought she'd never leave," Lisa hissed, ripping open her envelope.

"Kate's okay," said Shanon. "She has a lot of hidden talents. She's a good writer, she's musical, she reads Greek—"

"Spare me the list of her good points," Lisa broke in. "She's too much of everybody's big sister." She scanned the letter from Rob and drew in a breath.

"Listen to this!"

Dear Lisa,

We got your clever invitation. Your drawings are really funny. And we are all coming—

"They're coming!" Shanon cried.
"Fantastic," said Amy.
"Listen to the rest," Lisa went on.

Be ready to break out of prison, baby, because I plan to make the most complicated, convincing snow sculpture that has ever been made at Alma Stephens. I am an expert at this. Funny that you should want to do it, too. We should make a plan as to what we want to do. There's a lot of work involved; we will have to spend all day together in the freezing snow. That is, if it ever does snow. If it doesn't snow, we'll have to pack it in and watch ice hockey or maybe go back to your common room and watch E.T. on the VCR with all the lights out. That way it will be like a movie theater. I know I am goofing off with you. Don't be mad. I can't wait to come over and see you again.

Rob

P.S. Everybody has their own idea of what the Abominable Snowman looks like—a gigantic, ugly-looking cousin of Frosty the Snowman who really needs a haircut. Who knows? Maybe it's not like that at all. Maybe instead it's the Abominable SnowWOMAN! Can't a woman be over seven feet tall and have white fur all over her body? Why is it that this awesome monster has got to be a man?

Lisa squealed with laughter. "He's so funny! The Abominable Snowwoman! It sounds like some kind of character from a play! Wait!" she gasped. "There's something else inside the envelope!" She pulled it out and moaned. "It's his picture!"

Shanon and Amy each took in deep breaths, then crowded over to Lisa's side of the table. "Look at him!" Lisa gulped. "He's . . . he's so good-looking! Look at his curly hair—and his beautiful blue eyes!"

"He looks really tall there," said Shanon.

"He's a hunk all right," Amy agreed. "Especially in that sleeveless muscle shirt."

Shanon sat down again. "Now let me open my letter!" She tore open the envelope and took out a piece of notebook paper with Mars's writing. "It's cute," she murmured, scanning the letter.

"Read it out loud!" Lisa urged her.

"Okay," Shanon agreed.

Dear Shanon,

I will be there on the weekend of the 10th. I hope it's a clear night that Saturday. It's really getting close to the Solstice and that means it'll be one of the longest nights of the year. The stars will be visible the longest, too, if anybody's out there watching. I've checked cross-country in the afternoon. I'm glad you like that sport too. Write me back.

Mars

P.S. Make it snow why don't you? Also: very important— John Adams wants to have a private meeting with you over the computer on the Thursday after Thanksgiving at 8 p.m. sharp. He says to just get online with the Journalism Club. I guess he wants to talk to you about journalism.

That had better be it. I mean, I could get jealous. Anyway, he said it was important.

"Isn't that a nice letter?" said Shanon. "Look, Mars sent a picture, too!"

"It's sort of fuzzy," Lisa said, grabbing the photograph, "but you can still see what he looks like."

"He's got an interesting face!" said Amy.

"I love the way his hair falls into his eyes," said Shanon. "I've always liked guys with dark hair. And his eyes . . ."

"Intense!" agreed Amy.

A student waitress brought over their burgers.

"Well, that's great," Amy said bravely. "At least we know that all of them are coming. That's what Rob said anyway. And Rob and Mars want to do the same things that you wanted to do with them!"

Shanon and Lisa looked at each other. In their excitement they had forgotten all about Amy.

"I'm sure Simmie will be writing again too," Lisa said quickly.

"Right," said Shanon. "Simmie's letter will probably come in the mail tomorrow. I wouldn't worry."

Amy shrugged. "Oh, I'm not worried."

"I wonder why John Adams wants to talk to me over the computer," Shanon said, changing the subject. "If it's just about journalism, a lot of other kids get online from different schools next Monday."

"It is kind of curious," agreed Lisa. "Mars also said John wants the conversation to be private!"

"Mars *also* said he was jealous," teased Amy.

Shanon blushed. "Well he has nothing to be jealous

51

about. I barely know John. Maybe he really does just want to talk about journalism. After all, that's what we talked about last time."

Lisa's eyes got wider. "Unless," she whispered, "he wants to talk about Palmer."

"Why would he want to do that?" Shanon said. "He writes to her."

Lisa shrugged. "Maybe they had a fight or something. You're forgetting Palmer doesn't tell us anything anymore." She threw a sharp glance in their suitemate's direction. Palmer was still chatting with Germaine and hadn't even waved to them. "Let's not say a word about this to her," Lisa suggested spitefully.

"Maybe you're right," Shanon agreed. "Maybe if we keep a few secrets from Palmer, she'll start sharing with us again." She glanced at Amy. "What do you think?"

Amy shot a look toward Palmer and Germaine. "Why not?" she muttered. "John's writing to Palmer all the time. If he wants her to know what he talks to you about over the computer, I guess he'll tell her."

"Here she comes," Lisa hissed. "Now, remember, don't say anything!"

Germaine glided out of the snack bar as Palmer headed over to the three of them.

"Sorry I missed lunch with you all," she said, trying to sound natural. "Germaine and I were discussing our new ski outfits. We're ordering some things to wear at the Festival. By the way," she added, offhandedly, "did anybody get any letters?"

"I got one from Mars," Shanon said excitedly. "And Lisa got one from Rob. They're definitely coming!"

Palmer smiled. "Great! What about you, Amy?"

"Nothing from Simmie yet," Amy said flatly.

Two red spots appeared on Palmer's cheeks. "That's, uh, too bad," she said.

"What about you, Palmer?" Lisa demanded. "We're tired of telling you when we get mail since you never tell us. Is John coming to the Festival?"

"I'm sure he will," Palmer said with a shrug. "And if you're so interested in his letters, all you have to do is ask me what's in them."

"That's news to me," grumbled Lisa.

"Listen, we'd better go to French," Shanon said, looking at her watch. "Miss Grayson doesn't like us to be late."

"You're right," said Lisa. "Bye, Amy." Amy took Spanish instead of French.

Lisa, Shanon, and Palmer hurried off, leaving Amy nearly alone in the snack bar. She had another whole hour before her math class. Ordinarily she would have gone over to the gym for a while, but today she just didn't feel like it. She was disappointed that Simmie hadn't written to her. And she just couldn't figure out her roommate. Palmer was avoiding her more and more. And then there was her song. It still wasn't ready. Suddenly her life seemed about as dreary as a piece of old hamburger.

CHAPTER NINE

Dear Rob,

Hope you had a good Thanksgiving. We went to Shanon's house and there were five kinds of pie. I ate a slice of each one of them. There were so many people at the table that Shanon's dad had to put two tables together and it stretched into both the dining room and the living room. I wish I had a big family. There is just me and my brother Reggie in my family and my mom and dad and Gammy. My mom and dad were in Mexico and Gammy lives in this old age place, so Shanon asked me to go to her house and she also asked my brother Reggie which was neat of her.

Good news! Mr. Griffith liked my composition on an emotional experience very much—and I owe it all to you! Thanks for your suggestion about taking ideas from the newspaper. It really helped.

Your picture is great. Can't wait to see you in person.

Yours truly,
Lisa

P.S. Your idea about the Abominable Snowwoman cracks me up. But since nobody has really seen the thing close up, maybe we should call it *The Abominable Snow Person!* And, is this a good idea?! Let's do a sculpture of it for the snow sculpture event? This is a sketch of what it might look like. Write to let me know if you agree with this.

Dear Mars,
  I keep thinking about the image of all those stars and how they will be visible for so much longer near the Winter

Solstice. My dad told me that that is one way to make yourself feel better, to look up on a starry night and feel how small you are compared to the vast universe. Hope you had a nice Thanksgiving in St. Louis. I've signed us up for cross-country. I may have to do some work for The Ledger that day, too.

Sincerely,
Shanon

P.S. Thank you for your picture. I like it.

Dear Simmie,

How was your turkey day? I was at Shanon's with Lisa and Palmer. My folks were on a business trip in London and my grandmother went to Taiwan to visit relatives. So nobody would have been at home at my house. But it worked out because we don't always have turkey on Thanksgiving and I like turkey. Our cook at Alma who we call Mrs. Butter (her real name is Mrs. Worth) makes turkey hash and I'm the only one in the suite who will eat it. Mrs. Butter comes from Liverpool and always calls us "love" and stuffs everyone with all kinds of goodies. My roommate Palmer thinks she's dangerous because she encourages us to eat too much. But I think she's wonderful. I guess some things about Alma are growing on me, even though I miss New York.

Hate to brag, but I guess you heard about how we won the soccer championship in our league. It was an excellent final match! I'm sorry the season's over. I'm wondering if you ever wrote back to say what activity you are interested in for the Winter Festival weekend. Did you get my letter in which I said that I would like to get some *ice-skating in, possibly speed-skating? Lisa thinks your letter must have gotten lost because Rob wrote to her that all of The Unknown were coming. Anyway, would you write again so I can make sure and sign us up for some things?*

Yours truly,
Amy

"Are you sure I should write to him again?" Amy asked Lisa.

Lisa nodded. "Otherwise how are you going to know what activities he wants to do?"

Amy looked worried. "But maybe his letter didn't get lost. Maybe he didn't send one."

"Of course he sent one," Lisa insisted. "Didn't Rob say that all of The Unknowns were planning to come? Stop worrying, Amy. Simmie likes you."

"Remember the letter he sent you after the Halloween Mixer?" Shanon reminded her. "He said you were a cool dancer."

"And don't forget," Lisa added, "Simmie sent you that poster of himself. He wouldn't have done that if he wasn't serious—right?"

Amy folded the letter carefully and stuck it inside an envelope.

Dear Simmie,
By now you are probably wondering who I am. I can't tell you yet, but if you want to know more about me, my favorite food is lobster and my favorite place is the beach. My favorite car is a red jaguar. In fact I already own one,

only I am too young to drive it yet. My parents keep it in their garage.

I would like to have you come as my guest to the Winter Festival, but you must not tell anybody about it. If you agree to this, I will be waiting for you near the bottom of the down-hill ski trail at Brier Mt. on Saturday morning at ten o'clock. I will be wearing a yellow ski suit.

A secret admirer, "P"

P.S. If I were an animal, I'd be a lioness!
P.P.S. I hope it is not true what I'm hearing—that you have a girlfriend at Alma who is going to be your date.

"Oh, it's too good!" Germaine chuckled. "There's no way he'll be able to say no!"

Palmer giggled. "I hope the part about the car isn't too much. Suppose he finds out I'm lying?"

"There's no way he could find out," Germaine said impatiently. "You told him your parents keep it for you in Florida."

Palmer's eyes twinkled. "If this works, it'll be the most amazing thing I've ever done in my life."

"It's the work of a genius," Germaine agreed, smiling. "Of course, I have to take some of the credit."

"Oh, I would never have thought of it if you hadn't hinted that I should go after Simmie," Palmer added gratefully. "I just hope . . ." A cloud crossed her face.

"Don't tell me you're feeling guilty about your room-mate?" Germaine quipped. "The way this whole thing is planned, Amy Ho will never find out. It'll just seem like you ran into Simmie Randolph. And if he just happens to like you better, it won't be *your* fault."

Palmer smiled. "That's true. And I told Simmie not to

tell anybody about this. I don't think Amy will really care anyway."

Germaine shrugged. "What if she does? Anything's fair—remember?"

"Right," Palmer said doubtfully. "But even so, I really wouldn't do this if I wasn't so totally crazy about Simmie. It's like I just can't help myself." As Germaine nodded encouragement, a worried frown flashed across Palmer's face. "What if the yellow ski suit doesn't arrive on time?" she said.

"It'll get here," Germaine assured her. "By the way, I ordered one, too."

"Great," said Palmer. "What color?"

"Yellow," Germaine replied.

"But that way we'll be dressed in the same thing!" Palmer exclaimed.

"That's the idea," Germaine purred. "We're almost best friends, aren't we?"

"I guess it's okay," Palmer mumbled.

"It has to be okay," Germaine said, putting an arm around her shoulder. "I already ordered the ski suit."

"Which one of your Ardsley boyfriends is coming?" Palmer asked. Something about the way Germaine was acting made her uncomfortable.

"Oh, I haven't decided yet," Germaine replied carelessly. She picked up the letter Palmer had written to Simmie and licked the envelope. "Now," she instructed, handing it back to Palmer. "Go mail this."

Palmer trudged across the quad to the mailbox. She was so engrossed in thoughts of Simmie that she didn't hear the footsteps running up behind her.

"Hi, Palmer!"

Palmer started guiltily. "Hi, Amy," she replied.

"Is that a letter to John?" Amy asked.

Palmer slipped the letter she was holding into the mailbox before Amy could see the address. "Sure . . . it's a letter to John," she said nervously, pasting a smile on her face. "Is that a letter you're mailing to Simmie?"

Amy stepped up to the mailbox. "Yep, I wrote him again. His last letter must have gotten lost. I'm mailing Lisa's and Shanon's letters for them, too."

Palmer backed away from Amy. "That's nice of you. Well, I'd better go now."

"Where are you heading?" asked Amy. "Maybe we can walk together."

"I don't think so," Palmer said quickly. "I have to talk to Mr. Seganish about that history quiz. I guess I didn't do very well."

"No, that's not in the same direction," Amy said, disappointed. "I'm going over to the gym. I thought I'd get a swim in."

"In this weather?" Palmer exclaimed, shivering.

The girls looked at each other.

"I've been meaning to ask you," Amy began, "did I do something to make you mad at me?"

Palmer studied the toes of her boots. "Did you do something to me? Nope, not that I know of."

"I just thought I'd ask," muttered Amy. She turned toward the gym. "See you later."

"Sure," said Palmer. Watching Amy walk away, she felt bad for a moment. But it was too late to do anything about it. The letter to Simmie Randolph III was in the mail.

CHAPTER TEN

"*The world looks the same for a hundred days and the face of the mountain is covered* ..." Amy strummed and Brenda sang the words to Amy's new verse. "*If I could see, maybe I could recover and be free....*"

"Stop," said Amy, putting the guitar down. "I can't stand it."

"It sounds fine to me," Brenda argued, reaching for an open carton of milk. "I hear that milk makes your voice sound better."

"What difference will it make how your voice sounds if the song is bad?" moaned Amy.

"I know what!" Shanon chirped. She was huddled on the floor near the outlet, with her heating coil stuck in the teapot. "Why don't you put that Edna St. Vincent Millay poem we did in class to music?"

Amy shook her head. "That would be a different song from the one I'm thinking of." She turned to Brenda. "Maybe you should go back to the Springsteen."

"After all the work we've done on 'Cabin Fever'?" Brenda exclaimed.

"But if it's not ready to be in the show . . ." Amy argued. Shanon handed her a cup of instant hot chocolate, then gave one to Brenda.

"You still haven't told me who your guitar player is for Talent Night," Amy said to Brenda as they sipped their hot chocolate. "Whatever you're going to sing, you have to start practicing with her."

"I . . . I have to talk to you about that," Brenda said nervously. "I don't have one."

"What?" exclaimed Amy, almost spilling her drink.

"I thought I did," Brenda blurted out, "but then she couldn't do it and now you're the only one who can help me. Please, Amy!"

"I'm not playing my own song in front of a lot of people," Amy sputtered. "Don't worry, I'll get you another guitarist."

"Kate plays the guitar," Shanon said brightly. "Maybe she'll do it."

"I'm in trouble!" Lisa announced, bursting into the suite. "I've been accused of plagiarizing!"

"What?" gasped Shanon.

"I'll see you later," Brenda said, edging toward the door.

Lisa paced the room and Amy followed her. "Tell us what happened," Amy insisted, as soon as the Foxes were alone. "Who accused you?"

"It's not true, is it?" wailed Shanon.

Lisa stopped by the window. "I don't know!" she exploded. "All I know is Rob told me that he wrote a composition based on something he saw in the newspaper and then I did the same thing and—"

"You what?" Shanon chimed in.

"Rob did it, too!" Lisa insisted. "And nobody said he was cheating. But then Mr. Griffith showed my paper to some people in the English department and one of the other teachers had read the same story that I had and . . ." Hot tears fell down her face.

"That's horrible," Shanon said softly. "You mean you copied something and said it was yours?"

"Of course I didn't!" snapped Lisa. "I just used the idea of the story and pretended it happened to me as my emotional experience."

"It sounds to me like you might have plagiarized, all right," Amy said glumly. "What are they going to do to you?"

"I don't know. Mr. Griffith was kind of vague about it. He just said that this other teacher had read the article in the *Times* and that we would have to get together and talk about it. This is all Rob Williams's fault!"

"How can you say that?" said Shanon.

"Because he's the one who told me to do it," Lisa sputtered.

"But you're the one who did it," Shanon argued.

Lisa stood up. "I can't believe you're taking his side over mine!" she said, pacing furiously.

"Watch out!" Amy warned. "You're going to kick over the teapot—"

Lisa stumbled into the clay pot and knocked it against the corner. A dull crack sounded.

"Oh, no!" gasped Shanon. "You . . . you've broken it!" she said. "It's the teapot from my mother!"

"What was it doing on the floor?" Lisa exploded. "Anyway, it was an accident! I didn't mean to!"

"I know you didn't mean to," Shanon sniffed, bursting into tears, "but you did it anyway! It was something very special!" And gathering up the pieces of the pot, she fled to the bedroom.

Lisa groaned. "What else can go wrong?"

There was a soft knocking at the door. "I'm looking for Lisa," Miss Grayson said, sticking her head in. "Oh, there you are."

"Hi," Lisa said, flustered.

Miss Grayson saw the spilled water from the broken pot on the floor. Shanon's heating coil, still plugged in, was lying in the middle of it. "That looks dangerous," Miss Grayson warned.

"We had an accident," Amy said, hurrying to unplug the coil and wipe up the water.

Miss Grayson looked at Lisa. "I was wondering if you could come down to my apartment for a little talk."

Lisa gulped. "Right now?"

"If you're free," Miss Grayson replied. There was something in her tone of voice that made Lisa nervous.

"Okay, I can come now," said Lisa.

They left Amy alone in the sitting room. As she wiped up the last of the water, Palmer walked in looking radiant.

"It's snowing!" she cried. "It's really coming down! Look out the window!"

Amy jumped up. "Fantastic! Now we'll really have a Winter Festival!"

"Let's just hope this is a hard snow," Palmer said excitedly, "the kind that will pack down. Then we'll hope for a nice, fine powder for the weekend of the Festival."

"Are you and John definitely going in for downhill?" Amy asked.

"Well . . . I am," Palmer hedged. "I've ordered a yellow ski outfit that's to die for! There's no way that Sim—" She bit her lip and turned toward the window.

"Were you going to say something about Simmie?" asked Amy.

"Of course not," said Palmer, keeping her back to Amy. "Except that I was going to ask you if he'd written yet."

"Not yet," sighed Amy. "Maybe tomorrow."

Downstairs in Miss Grayson's quarters, Lisa nervously waited for the young teacher to speak. The cozy apartment smelled like flowers and oranges. Crammed bookshelves lined every wall. Miss Grayson sat in a big, worn armchair, while Lisa sat stiffly on the edge of the couch.

"Mr. Griffith told me about your composition," Miss Grayson began gently. "He's very perturbed."

Lisa hung her head. "I'm sorry."

Miss Grayson leaned forward. "I'm so surprised, Lisa. I can't believe you would cheat. There must be some explanation."

"There is," said Lisa. "I didn't know it would be cheating—honest! You see, a certain person told me that he had gotten an idea for a paper he wrote from the newspaper and I have such a hard time thinking of things to write about that I—"

"You didn't actually copy the article, did you?" Miss Grayson asked.

Lisa shook her head vigorously. "No, the whole story was mine word for word. It was about a baby who was found on a doorstep and taken to a hospital by this man. Then the nurses fell in love with the baby and took care of her. In the end the man ended up adopting her and the girl in the family was really excited."

"It's a nice story," said Miss Grayson. "Writers are often inspired to write about things that happened to other people."

Lisa hung her head. "I guess that's what Mr. Griffith is upset about. I wrote the story as if it really happened . . . to me."

"I don't understand," said Miss Grayson.

"I was the sister of the house," Lisa explained. "I wrote the story as if my father was the one who found the baby on his doorstep. When I read the article . . . it was a really emotional experience."

Miss Grayson's eyes lit up with understanding. "How interesting! And did you think you were doing something dishonest when you wrote the story as if it were something that actually happened to you?"

Lisa flushed. "I thought it might be a little bit dishonest. But really . . . when I read the newspaper story I almost started crying. I wished that my father had been the one to find that little baby and that I . . ."

Her voice trailed off and a tear trickled down her cheek. Miss Grayson offered her a handkerchief. "It was a stupid thing to do, wasn't it?" Lisa said softly.

"You did misrepresent the events," Miss Grayson admitted.

Lisa blew her nose. "What's going to happen to me?" she asked miserably. "There must be a big punishment for plagiarizing."

"I wouldn't classify what you did as plagiarizing exactly," Miss Grayson told her.

Lisa looked hopeful. "You mean I'm not in trouble?"

Miss Grayson got up to stir the fire. A spark flew onto the rose-colored rug and she stamped it out. "That's up to Mr. Griffith," she answered. "I suggest you go and tell him what you've told me. You may not be guilty of plagiarizing, but you really didn't do the assignment properly. Mr. Griffith wanted you to write about something you really experienced."

"And I sort of borrowed somebody else's experience," Lisa said humbly. "If only I hadn't been dumb enough to listen to this friend of mine and look in the newspaper," she muttered.

Miss Grayson busied herself with the tea kettle. "Making mistakes is the way we grow," she said. "But it's important to face up to them."

Lisa sniffed. "That's why I have to talk to Mr. Griffith."

"Precisely," Miss Grayson said, smiling. "Let's have some tea, shall we? I want to hear more about why you were so moved about this news story. . . ."

Dear Rob,
  I am sorry that I thanked you before for that idea of yours to get stories out of the newspaper. Thanks to that, I am now in trouble. Who knows, I might not even be able to go to the Festival because of this. So, thanks for nothing.
                                    Sincerely,
                                    Lisa McGreevy

CHAPTER ELEVEN

"Look at it!" shouted Amy. "It's incredible!"

"The whole world looks like it's covered with a blanket of snow," sighed Shanon.

Lisa picked up a handful of powder and licked it. "Ummm, maybe we can make snow ice cream with some of that cocoa."

"Watch me make an angel!" laughed Palmer. Giddily, she threw herself onto the ground and spread her arms out. And when she got up her rabbit-fur coat was caked with snow.

Amy's eyes twinkled. "Pretty good angel for somebody raised in Florida."

"Snow does something to me," Palmer laughed.

The four of them stood still in the middle of the quadrangle while fat feathers of snow continued to pour down from the eerie white sky.

"What did Mr. Griffith say?" Shanon asked Lisa. The two girls hadn't spoken much to each other since Lisa had broken the teapot.

"He's giving me a second chance," replied Lisa. "I have a week to write about an emotional experience that really happened to me."

"This is an emotional experience right now!" cried Amy, spinning around. "Let's have a snowball fight! That'll be something to write about!" She slung a handful of powder at Lisa.

"Eeek!" Lisa squealed, dodging. "You're never going to make anything hard enough to throw out of this stuff!"

"Who says?" Shanon challenged, giggling. Digging up a big chunk, she threw it at Lisa's head. Powder fell all over her ski cap.

"Okay, you asked for it!" Lisa laughed, hurling a spray of snow at Shanon, then at Palmer.

"Hey, watch it!" Palmer yelled cheerfully. She took two handfuls of snow and threw them at Amy. Amy grabbed a big chunk and aimed at her head. Palmer ducked and Lisa got her from behind.

"Come on, Shanon!" Amy cried. "You be on my side!" Lisa and Palmer lined up on the other side and the four girls began to do battle.

"Got you!" Amy yelled, zinging Palmer.

"Got you back!" Palmer replied. She missed and fell laughing into a snow bank. "Help! Get me out of here!"

"Leave her there!" cried Shanon. She ran up and put some snow down Lisa's collar, while Amy pummeled the helpless Palmer. All four of them were laughing.

"Time out!" called Lisa, brushing the snow out of her coat.

Amy and Shanon helped Palmer out of the snow bank. "That was fun," Palmer said breathlessly.

The four girls looked at each other. The moment had a magical feel to it.

"Hey, Palmer!" They turned to see Germaine across the quadrangle. Palmer waved.

"Come on!" Germaine called loudly. "Let's go check for our packages!"

Palmer snapped to attention. "I've got to go," she said quickly. "You see, Germaine and I ordered these new ski outfits and—"

"Why do you have to go now?" Amy said firmly. "We were going to get some hot chocolate."

"How can we have chocolate?" Palmer shrugged. "Lisa broke Shanon's teapot."

Shanon looked away and Lisa winced.

"We were going to the snack bar for it," Amy insisted.

"Well, sorry," Palmer said. "Germaine is calling me."

"And is Germaine Richards so important?" Amy challenged angrily.

"Well . . . she's my friend," Palmer sputtered.

"So are we!" Amy declared.

Palmer looked torn for a moment. "Don't be childish," she finally huffed.

"Childish!" Lisa chimed in. "You're the one who acts like a spoiled brat all the time."

"Come on, Palmer!" Germaine cried out shrilly.

Palmer began to walk away and Amy grabbed her arm. "How come you don't want to be with us?" she asked. "You're one of the Foxes."

"Maybe I don't want to be one of the Foxes anymore," Palmer mumbled. She looked over her shoulder at the impatient Germaine and then back at Amy.

"You used to think the Foxes was a good idea," Shanon said sadly, "especially when we got pen pals."

70

"That's the whole reason I don't like the Foxes anymore," snapped Palmer. "If it hadn't been for the fact that I got John Adams . . . Oh never mind!" she sputtered, running away.

Amy picked up a snowball and took aim. She threw it hard, hitting Palmer in the shoulder.

"Ouch!" Palmer cried, glaring back at her. "That hurt."

Amy only stared. Tears of anger filled her eyes as Palmer took off with Germaine.

Amy, Shanon, and Lisa had their hot chocolate and then returned to their suite to do homework and study. They'd been working intensely for two hours when Lisa finally broke the silence.

"I can't think of a new topic," she sighed, exhausted. She'd been struggling with the composition for Mr. Griffith while Shanon read her Latin assignment and Amy went over math problems at the sitting-room desk.

"I'm sure something will come to you," muttered Shanon. Even though they'd had fun in the snow, she was still mad about the broken teapot.

After a few more minutes of silence, Amy went into the bedroom to get a sweater and Lisa threw down her notebook with a sigh. Turning to Shanon she said, "Listen, I'm sorry about your teapot. I really am."

"It's broken now," Shanon pointed out. "I don't want to talk about it."

"I promise to make it up to you," Lisa went on. "If you like, you can have anything you want from my half of the closet."

Shanon blinked. "Really?"

71

"Even my new gypsy skirt," said Lisa. "Or how about my pink striped bike pants?"

Shanon smiled in spite of herself. "Bike pants can't take the place of a teapot."

"But you'd look great in them," Lisa said earnestly. "And it would make me feel better. It's bad enough having Mr. Griffith mad at me without being on the outs with you, too."

"Let's forget about it," Shanon said. "The teapot's broken. It's over."

"I really felt awful when I broke it," Lisa added quietly. "Maybe I should write about that as an emotional experience. I was afraid that you'd be so angry that we wouldn't be friends anymore."

"Don't be silly," said Shanon. "It's only a teapot. Friendships are more important than those kind of things."

"I'll make you a new teapot at the pottery studio," Lisa said brightly.

"You haven't even finished those mugs," Shanon reminded her.

"I'll finish them," Lisa said determined. "And I'll make the teapot, too! If you'll just accept my apology."

Shanon smiled. "Okay. You're forgiven, even if you never make the new teapot."

When Palmer returned to their room that evening, Amy gave her the cold shoulder. Palmer pretended not to notice and settled back on her bed to read a fashion magazine.

"I've been thinking," Amy said finally. "If you want to have Germaine as a roommate instead of me, it's okay."

72

Palmer looked shocked. "Germaine has a single room. She wouldn't want a roommate."

"Oh," said Amy. "I just wanted you to know that I wouldn't have hurt feelings."

"Do you want another roommate?" Palmer asked her. Amy shrugged. "Nope."

"Listen . . ." Palmer blurted out, "I know you think I'm different. I mean I'm not a jock or a musician or smart in English like Shanon. And I—"

"What does that have to do with being different?" Amy broke in, puzzled. "Anyway, you're the one who thinks I'm different."

Palmer's face reddened. "You're right. I do. But you think I'm stupid."

"No, I don't," Amy protested. "I think you're a cool person."

Palmer wrinkled her nose in disbelief. "You do?"

"Don't ask me why," sighed Amy.

Palmer glanced at the poster of Simmie and her heart pounded. "You're not in love with Simmie Randolph, are you?" she asked. She was hoping that it wouldn't matter all that much to Amy that she was stealing her pen pal.

Amy giggled. "In love? I like him. But I hardly know him. How could I love him? Anyway, love is too deep for somebody my age."

"It's not too deep for me!" exclaimed Palmer. Every time she looked at Simmie's poster, she was sure she knew what the feeling was. "But anyway," she added quietly, "I'm glad you're not in love with Simmie."

"You're not in love with John, are you?" Amy asked. Palmer rolled her eyes. "Of course not."

73

"How come you never let us read the letters he writes to you?" Amy asked.

"You want to read one?" Palmer said carelessly. She crossed to her bureau drawer and tossed John's latest letter in Amy's direction. He hadn't mentioned the fact that Palmer hadn't been writing to him. Not directly anyway.

"Can I read it?" Amy asked.

Palmer shrugged. "Sure. I've got to read some of this junk for history. If I don't pass the next quiz, Seganish is going to report me to Miss Pryn."

Amy opened the letter. The words in John's neat handwriting leaped out at her.

Dear Palmer,
This is my latest. It is the only way I have of expressing to you how I feel.

Crime of passion not committed, I'm just sitting here
About to write you my life's story
Been restless all day through
I'm going to break through like the sun at dawn, have fun
Near winter's fire
Forever your name will be emblazed in my brain
Even if I don't see you
Verge of fears, surge of tears, but I won't be sorry
Every girl will have your face, so I must get started
Run a mile through acid snow cures my restless sorrow

You probably won't understand this any more than you understood any of my other stuff. But I'm sending it anyway. Just chalk it up as the rantings of a mad football player. But look at the first letter in each line and you'll know how I feel.

74

"Did you look at the first letter in each line?" Amy asked, putting the letter down.

Palmer looked up sleepily from her book. "Huh?"

Amy grinned. "It says *cabin fever*. That's just what I've been writing about. As a matter of fact, there are some lines I'd like to steal from this poem for my song."

Palmer perked up. "Why don't you just take them? John will never find out."

"He'll find out when he comes to the Festival," said Amy. "Anyway, I'm not going to do anything like that. Especially after what happened to Lisa with that newspaper article."

Palmer's blue eyes opened wide. "I know what! Why don't you write to him?"

"To who?" asked Amy.

"To John!" Palmer said excitedly. "I wouldn't mind! And I'm sure he wouldn't. You could ask permission to use some of his poem for the song you're writing."

"But John's *your* pen pal," Amy said doubtfully.

"I don't mind," Palmer said. "Honest!"

Amy looked thoughtfully at John's letter. "Well, maybe I'll just write to ask permission about the poem. I really think I could use some of this."

Palmer beamed. If Amy was writing to John, she wouldn't have to feel guilty at all about writing to Simmie. "Write to him, right away!" she said.

"Okay," Amy agreed. "I will."

Settling back to her history book, Palmer looked up at Simmie's poster. Everything was going to be just perfect.

Dear John,
 Palmer said it would be okay if I wrote to you. I read

75

your latest poem and I really like it. It's an amazing coincidence, because I am writing a song about Cabin Fever. (Simmie may have told you this.) And I see the acrostic to your poem is "cabin fever" as well. Not too odd considering how cooped up we all are in winter. Can't wait until Winter Festival. Anyway, I am wondering if I might use part of the poem you wrote for my song on cabin fever. I would tell everybody that some of the lyrics are yours of course. I have pretty good verses, but was having trouble with the chorus. Please write back and let me know.

Thank you,
Amy Ho

P.S. Please say hi to Simmie. I haven't gotten his answer to my letter. Please ask him to let me know what activity he would like to do at the Festival if he is still coming. Thank you.

CHAPTER TWELVE

"I got a letter from Simmie!" Amy announced, running into the suite. "Where's Palmer?"

"I don't know," Lisa said glumly.

"Well, where's Shanon, then?" asked Amy. "I want to open this."

Lisa smiled weakly. "You can open it with me. I've got a letter, too, from Rob."

Amy got down on the floor next to Lisa. They were sitting with their backs resting against the loveseat. "You go first," Lisa prodded.

"Okay," Amy agreed. "First I'll open this one."

"You got two letters?" Lisa asked.

Amy nodded. "One from Simmie and one from John Adams. I asked about using part of his song, remember? I sure hope he said yes." She studied the two envelopes for a moment before tearing John's open. "I think I'll read this one first," she added, "and save the best—Simmie's—for last."

Dear Amy,

I am flattered and very excited that you like my poem. Funny that you are writing a song on the same theme. You know what they say about great minds being in the same places? Anyway, please feel free to use whatever you need for the lyrics. It would have been fun to hear it on Talent Night. But good luck.

Yours truly,
John Adams

P.S. I passed your message on to Simmie. Please remind Shanon about the Journalism Club.

"What a nice letter," Amy exclaimed.

"How come he says he's not going to get to hear the song?" asked Lisa.

Amy shrugged.

Lisa stared at her letter from Rob. "I can't keep putting this off," she said. "I wrote him such a nasty letter last time. He's probably mad at me." She tore at the envelope.

"I'm going to read mine from Simmie at the same time," Amy said, busy with her own envelope. "I can't wait any longer."

"Ugh," Lisa murmured as she scanned her letter. "This is awful."

"Mine, too," Amy whispered. Her face had a stunned expression and she was fighting back tears.

"But Simmie had nothing to be angry with you about!" exclaimed Lisa. "What did he say?"

The girls exchanged letters.

"Yep, awful," Amy mumbled in agreement, reading Lisa's letter from Rob. "He's really mad at you."

"And this letter Simmie wrote to you is mean and

ridiculous!" steamed Lisa. "Did you ever tell anyone that you were his girlfriend?"

Amy shook her head "no."

"I didn't think so," said Lisa. "What a jerk! He doesn't even know how to spell the word *friend* correctly."

"He never did know how to spell," Amy said with a swallow.

They laid down the letters and looked at each other.

"Neither of us has a date now," Amy said dully. "What are we going to do?"

"I don't know," wailed Lisa. "Right now I feel like crawling into bed and never coming out." She balled Rob's letter up and threw it against the bookshelf. "Take that, Rob Williams!" she shouted.

Crumpling Simmie's letter, Amy shot a basket into the trash can. "And so much for Simmie Randolph the Third!" she quipped bravely. The girls dragged off to their bedrooms, leaving their letters behind them.

Dear Lisa,

I was flabbergasted to get your letter. Don't blame your problems with your English teacher on me. The ideas I got out of the newspapers I only used as inspirations and I told the teachers up front that I was doing that. Anyway, don't count on me to help you make the Abominable Snowperson. I'm sure you can do a good job of that by yourself.

Robert Williams

Dear Amy,

I do not appreciate your passing messages to me in your letter to John. I do not intend to do any skating at the Winter Festival. That's why I didn't write back to you.

79

There is someone else that I have planned to spend time with who likes skiing. Hope this does not hurt your feelings, but I got pretty mad when I heard that you were passing it around that you were my girlfreind. Best of luck. Maybe I will run into you anyway.

Simmie Randolph III

CHAPTER THIRTEEN

"It's dark in here!" whispered Lisa as she and Shanon stuck their heads into the *Ledger* office.

"We'd better not turn on too many lights," said Shanon. "Kate may be walking by and notice." She settled herself quickly at the computer, flicked a couple of switches, and started typing on the keyboard.

"I wish I knew how one of these things worked," said Lisa, peering over her shoulder. "What are you doing?"

"Right now, I'm typing in *The Ledger*'s ID number and password," Shanon mumbled. "Then I'll get online with the Journalism Club."

"And John will talk with you?"

"If he's online like he said he'd be," Shanon answered. "It's exactly eight o'clock. . . . I really shouldn't be doing this," she added guiltily. "The school pays for this service so the newspaper staff can improve its journalism."

"Journalism might be all that John wants to talk about," Lisa argued.

"True," Shanon grunted. "But *we* want to talk about other things—right?"

Lisa jutted her chin out. "Right! Like Rob Williams and Simmie Randolph."

"John's online!" Shanon whispered excitedly. "I see his code number for the Ardsley Lit. Mag. in one of the Journalism Club conference rooms."

"What's that?" asked Lisa. The numbers on the computer screen made no sense to her.

"A conference room is just a code you punch into the computer so you can talk to someone online," replied Shanon. She sent a message over the keyboard.

/SEN 99 ARDSLEY LIT. MAG. IDENTIFY YOURSELF. ARE YOU AN UNKNOWN? /GA

"What's all that stuff you typed at the beginning and end?" hissed Lisa.

"The first part means send me number ninety-nine," Shanon explained hastily. "Ninety-nine is the number for the Lit. Mag. today. 'GA' means 'go ahead.' If John has gotten my message, he'll send me an answer."

A response flashed across the screen. OKAY. UNKNOWN JOHN ADAMS IN JOURNALISM CLUB CONFERENCE ROOM TWO. IDENTIFY YOURSELF. ARE YOU A FOX? /GA

OKAY. YES. IT'S SHANON DAVIS ONLINE WITH YOU. WE'D BETTER MAKE THIS QUICK. MY EDITOR DOESN'T KNOW I'M USING THE COMPUTER. SHE'D KILL ME. /GA

OKAY, SHANON. SAME GOES FOR THE LIT. MAG. EDITOR. BUT I HAD TO TALK TO YOU PRIVATELY. /GA

OKAY, JOHN. ABOUT WHAT? /GA

"Why do you keep writing 'okay'?" Lisa whispered.

"It's computer language for 'I read you.' "

Another message from John flashed across the screen, and he and Shanon continued their computer conversation.

OKAY, SHANON. HERE GOES—I NEED INFORMATION ABOUT YOUR SUITEMATE PALMER. /GA

OKAY, WHAT KIND OF INFO? /GA

OKAY, DOES SHE HAVE A BOYFRIEND? /GA

Lisa and Shanon looked at each other. "How come he's asking that?" said Lisa. Shanon shrugged and keyed in:

OKAY, I DON'T THINK SO. WHY DO YOU ASK? /GA

OKAY, BECAUSE SHE DOES NOT WRITE TO ME ANYMORE. /GA

OKAY, THAT'S IMPOSSIBLE. SHE INVITED YOU TO THE FESTIVAL! RIGHT? /GA

WRONG! SHE DIDN'T. DO YOU KNOW WHO SHE IS INVITING INSTEAD? /GA

Shanon paused. "I don't understand," she said to Lisa. "We included all of them on the invitation."

"But then we were supposed to invite them individually," Lisa reminded her. "Maybe Palmer didn't do that!"

"But why not?" exclaimed Shanon.

She keyed in again: JOHN, THIS IS TOTALLY RANDOM TO US; WE THOUGHT PALMER HAD INVITED YOU. /GA

"Ask about Rob!" Lisa interrupted.

"What do you want to know?" Shanon whispered.

"Ask if he's still mad at me," Lisa blurted desperately. "No! Ask if he's still planning to come to the Festival!"

Shanon typed. JOHN, IS ROB WILLIAMS COMING TO THE FESTIVAL? /GA

SHANON, NO HE IS NOT. I AM NOT GOING EITHER! /GA

Lisa groaned. "This is horrible. Now none of us will have dates!"

HOW'S MARS? Shanon typed in quickly. IS HE COMING TO THE FESTIVAL? /GA

OKAY, MARS IS COMING. /GA

"Thank goodness," breathed Shanon. She glanced over her shoulder. "Maybe we'd better sign off, Lisa."

"No, let's ask about Simmie first," Lisa said quickly.

Suddenly the overhead light flashed on in the office. "What are you two doing in the dark?" a voice grumbled.

Shanon swiveled around in alarm. Kate was standing in the doorway.

"Hi there," Lisa squeaked nervously.

"Hi yourself," Kate replied suspiciously.

Shanon blushed. "I was, that is, we were just . . ." She glanced back at the computer.

John's message flashed across the screen. FOX, ARE YOU STILL THERE? DID YOU ASK ME A QUESTION? /GA

OKAY, I'M HERE! Shanon keyed in frantically. JUST A MINUTE! I THINK I'M IN TROUBLE!

"What are you doing on the computer?" Kate said, leaning in to read John's message.

"She's working on a newspaper story," fibbed Lisa. "With the Journalism Club."

"What kind of story?" Kate demanded of Shanon. "Who told you to go online with the Journalism Club?"

"Well . . . I . . . you see, John Adams works on the Ardsley Lit. Mag and . . ." Her face turned pale. She wasn't able to lie well. "I'm in a conference room with him right now," she confessed. "Just let me finish the conversation."

"You mean you're having private conversations with the newspaper's computer," exploded Kate. "When Dolores hears about this—"

"But she won't unless you tell her," pleaded Shanon as another message from John flashed across the screen:

FOX, ARE YOU READY TO SIGN OFF YET? /GA

OKAY, NOT YET!! answered Shanon.

"Just let her finish, Kate," begged Lisa. "This Journalism Club thing is really neat. I mean . . . you can get people on the computer and not just talk about journalism."

"How did you know he was going to be online?" Kate asked curiously.

"We planned it ahead of time," Shanon replied, desperately. "Please, I'll tell you about it later!"

"Ask about Simmie now," urged Lisa, pushing past Kate.

OKAY, UNKNOWN, WE WANT TO ASK YOU ABOUT SIMMIE RANDOLPH III, Shanon typed. /GA

OKAY, FOX. WHAT ABOUT RANDOLPH III? /GA

OKAY, WHO IS HE MEETING AT THE FESTIVAL? WE HEAR HE IS HANGING WITH SOMEONE OTHER THAN AMY. /GA

FOX, I DON'T KNOW. SOME MYSTERY GIRL FROM ALMA HAS INVITED HIM. /GA

OKAY, DO YOU KNOW WHO SHE IS? /GA

OKAY, SHANON. NO. NEITHER DOES SIMMIE. BUT SOME GIRL HAS BEEN WRITING HIM AND HE IS IN LOVE WITH HER! /GA

"Incredible!" gasped Lisa. "Somebody stole our pen-pals idea!"

"And then she stole Simmie," breathed Shanon.

"Ask him about the girl!" Lisa insisted. "He must know something about her!"

OKAY, UNKNOWN. DO YOU KNOW ANYTHING AT ALL ABOUT THE MYSTERY ALMA GIRL? /GA

NO, FOX. SIMMIE DOESN'T EITHER. BUT SHE HAS ALL THIS STUFF IN COMMON WITH HIM. THEY HAVE THE SAME FAVORITE COLOR AND FOOD AND THE SAME FAVORITE CAR; SHE WOULD ALSO BE THE SAME ANIMAL IF SHE WERE AN ANIMAL. HE'S SUPPOSED TO MEET HER AT BRIER MT. SKI SLOPE THE WEEKEND OF THE FESTIVAL. ANYTHING ELSE YOU WANT TO KNOW? /GA

YES! WHAT DOES THE GIRL LOOK LIKE? Shanon punched in furiously. /GA

OKAY, SHE'LL BE WEARING A YELLOW SKI SUIT, came John's answer.

"Ask him something else," Lisa said breathlessly.

UNKNOWN, DON'T YOU KNOW ANYTHING MORE? Shanon typed. WHAT IS HER NAME? /GA

OKAY, FOX. WE DON'T KNOW HER NAME. BUT SHE SIGNS HER LETTERS "P." /GA

"You'd better sign off now," Kate warned, breathing down Shanon's neck. "Dolores and I are having an editorial meeting here in five minutes.

"Yikes," said Shanon. "Why didn't you tell me?"

"Sign off," Lisa said flatly. "We've got all we need anyway."

THANKS, UNKNOWN! Shanon wrote. SORRY I COULDN'T BE MORE HELP. /GA

OKAY, FOX, John wrote back. THANK YOU! SAY HI TO AMY!

Shanon typed in the word EXIT and shut down the computer.

"Pretty nifty trick," Kate said, giving her an accusing look.

"I'm sorry," Shanon mumbled desperately. "I know I shouldn't have used the newspaper computer this way, but there were some things we had to discuss and—"

"We'll only do this again in extreme emergencies," Lisa promised.

"You'll do this again never," said Kate firmly. "I have to admit it's a cool idea though. In fact, my boyfriend has a computer in his room. Maybe I . . ." she looked at Lisa and stopped herself.

"You mean *you* have a boyfriend?" Lisa blurted out in a shocked voice.

"How nice," Shanon cut in, trying to cover Lisa's blunder. "Does he go to Ardsley?"

Kate's face reddened. "Yes, as a matter of fact he does," she confessed, avoiding Lisa's stare. "But we haven't told many people that we're going together."

"We won't tell a soul that you have a boyfriend," Lisa said smoothly, "if you don't tell how we used the computer."

Kate shrugged. "All right, I'll keep quiet about it. For now, anyway."

* * *

"That was close!" said Lisa as they headed back to Fox Hall. "There are more mysteries going on between Alma and Ardsley than I care to count. Now even Kate Majors has a boyfriend. What kind of a boy would like her? Must be a dweeb."

"I'm more interested in Simmie Randolph's mystery date," said Shanon. "I wonder who she is."

"I've got a pretty good idea," Lisa muttered. "All I need is one more piece of evidence."

"There's not much to go on," said Shanon.

"Oh, there's a lot to go on," Lisa disagreed. "John said that the mysterious Miss P knew all kinds of stuff about Simmie, his favorite color, his favorite food, even what animal he would be."

Shanon giggled. "Reminds me of that questionnaire we sent The Unknown."

Lisa nodded knowingly. "Exactly!"

CHAPTER FOURTEEN

"How can you be so sure it's Palmer?"

"Who else could know all that stuff Simmie wrote on the questionnaire?" argued Lisa. "And remember that time Palmer asked to see the folder where we keep all the stuff from The Unknown?"

"She said she was looking at John's questionnaire," said Shanon.

"But Simmie's was in there, too!" Lisa exclaimed.

Shanon shook her head. "I just can't believe that anybody would be so sneaky. Not even Palmer."

"I bet Palmer still has that folder in her room!" Lisa said, scanning the bottom bookshelf. "It's not here, anyway."

Lisa turned and stalked into Amy and Palmer's room.

"What are you going to do?" Shanon asked, hanging outside the doorway.

"I'm going to find that folder," Lisa declared. "It's property of the Foxes and Palmer should have returned it." She shuffled through the stack of books and papers on Palmer's desk. "Here it is!" The folder was stuck in a magazine. Lisa leafed through it. "Look at this!" she said triumphantly.

Shanon crept closer. "What is it?"

"It's Simmie's questionnaire," Lisa said. "Somebody's circled all kinds of stuff with a pencil!"

"I see what you mean," Shanon gulped, peering over Lisa's shoulder. "But maybe it wasn't Palmer who did that. Maybe Amy—"

"Hi, you all!" Palmer sang out gaily. Shanon jumped and Lisa quickly shut the folder.

Palmer came into the room carrying a big box. "I got my new ski suit in the mail!" she exclaimed. "I can't wait to open it up. Want to see?"

"Yes, I'd like to see it," Lisa said, steaming.

"What's the matter with you?" Palmer asked, wrestling with the tape on the box. "Still in trouble about that story you wrote?"

"I'm taking care of that, thank you," Lisa replied curtly.

Palmer got the box open. "Oh, it's beautiful!" she squealed, catching sight of the ski suit. "It looks even better than in the catalogue. Wait until Germaine sees it! She ordered one just like it, you know."

Palmer pulled the suit out of the box and held it up in front of her. Shanon took in a sharp breath and Lisa's eyes narrowed.

"It's yellow," Shanon said quietly.

"It sure is," Lisa added grimly.

"It's my favorite color!" Palmer said brightly.

Shanon and Lisa both glared at her.

"It's Simmie Randolph's favorite color too!" Lisa said, pointing to the folder.

"What are you doing with that?" Palmer asked uncomfortably.

"What were *you* doing with it?" accused Lisa.

The back of Palmer's neck felt hot. "I was looking over John's questionnaire," she said, trying to sound natural.

"You're such a liar, Palmer Durand," Shanon blurted out.

"Who are you calling a liar?" Palmer cried. "And how come you're in my room snooping around, anyway?"

"We came in here because we were looking for The Unknown's folder," Lisa said indignantly. "It's the property of the Foxes—all of the Foxes, not just one of us."

"Why be so picky about it?" Palmer said nonchalantly. "It's not like I wasn't going to return it."

"Yeah, you were going to return it all right," said Lisa. "After you got all kinds of information about Simmie so you could write letters to him!"

Palmer's face turned crimson. "I . . . I don't know what you're talking about," she stammered, grabbing the ski suit. "I'm going to Germaine's room."

"Just a minute," Lisa said, blocking her way.

"I called up John through the Journalism Club last night," Shanon said. "We know that you haven't been writing to him."

"And we also know that Simmie Randolph has some mystery date for the Winter Festival who's going to wear a yellow ski suit!" cut in Lisa.

"What difference does that make?" Palmer sputtered. "Anybody could wear a yellow ski suit!"

"Anybody with the initial 'P'?" Lisa persisted.

Palmer's lip trembled and she began to breathe hard.

"Okay, so I wrote to Simmie," she confessed. "It's a free country, isn't it?"

"How could you be so sneaky?" cried Lisa.

"And so mean?" added Shanon. "Poor Amy! Think how she'll feel when she finds out her own roommate—"

"Don't tell Amy," Palmer pleaded.

"How do you expect to keep it from her?" said Lisa.

"That's right," Shanon said. "What do you think she'll think when she sees you and Simmie hanging out together at the Festival? He already told her he has another date!"

"I don't know what she'll think," Palmer said desperately. "Maybe she'll just think I bumped into Simmie and he liked me. Maybe she'll think that's all there is to it."

"Amy's not dumb," said Lisa. "Anyway, don't you have any kind of conscience? You stole Amy's pen pal!"

"That's all Simmie was to her!" Palmer argued. "She doesn't even care that much that they're not writing! She told me herself that she wasn't in love with him!"

They heard the door to the suite open.

"It's her," Lisa said grimly. "You'd better tell her, Palmer."

Palmer groaned. "I can't. She'll be so mad."

"If you don't tell her," Shanon said boldly, "we will."

Amy strolled into the bedroom. "My dad sent me some new speed skates," Amy announced cheerfully. "And look what else I've got!" She held out a cylindrical package.

Palmer grinned weakly. "I guess today's the day for packages."

Amy smiled. "Is that your new ski suit? It's nice."

"Yeah, it's yellow," Lisa muttered, giving Palmer a dirty look.

"How come you're all standing around?" Amy asked,

crossing to the desk. She got some scissors and slit the tape off the top of the cylinder.

"There's something I guess I have to tell you," Palmer said, swallowing hard. Beads of perspiration broke out on her forehead. "I think I'm going to be sick."

"Don't tell me you're getting the flu!" exclaimed Amy.

"Oh, that's not why she's sick," said Lisa coldly.

Amy pulled a rolled-up poster out of the package. "Guess what this is!" she said triumphantly.

Shanon gulped. "Another poster of Simmie?"

"Yuk, no," said Amy, "but I ordered it from the same company he got his from." She unfurled a big blow-up of the Foxes and held it in front of her.

"Wow," said Lisa.

"It's from that picture Kate took of us," said Shanon softly.

"It looks fantastic," Palmer choked, feeling miserable.

"Well, don't everybody jump up and down about it," Amy said, lowering the poster so they could see her face. She spread it out on her bed. Lisa had worn a red turtleneck and big earrings, Amy was in her usual black, Shanon in pink, and Palmer in pale-blue lace. "Don't we look incredible?" crowed Amy. "I think I'm going to take down my Joan Jett poster and hang this up!"

Lisa looked at Palmer again.

"Palmer has something to tell you," Shanon said. "Don't you, Palmer?"

Amy looked at Palmer, too. "Well, what is it?"

"I don't know how to say this. . . ." Palmer squirmed. Before, writing to Simmie hadn't seemed so awful, but now that she was forced to confess . . .

"Go ahead, Palmer," Lisa prodded.

Palmer took a breath. "I'm the one Simmie is going to hang out with at the Festival!" she blurted out quickly.

Amy blinked. "I don't get it. I thought he made a date with someone else."

"It's me," gulped Palmer. "I've . . . I've been writing to him . . . behind your back."

Amy stared at her roommate for a minute and then a puzzled grin flashed across her face. "This is some kind of joke, right?"

"No . . . it's not," sputtered Palmer. "I mean . . . I don't know what I mean. You didn't really seem to like the guy, and . . ."

Amy's face darkened. She looked as if she would explode, but all she did was grab her jacket and head for the door.

"Wait!" Palmer cried. "Aren't you even going to say anything?"

"Yes!" Amy snapped over her shoulder. "I hate you!"

CHAPTER FIFTEEN

It wasn't easy being hated. Every morning when she got up, all Palmer could see was Amy's back. Her roommate had refused to even look at her. And Shanon and Lisa were acting almost as cold. At breakfast and lunch they hardly spoke to her, and nobody waited for her anymore after classes.

That's it, thought Palmer, *I'm out of the Foxes.* She glanced at the poster of all four of them; Amy had taken down Joan Jett and hung it up. *Well, I never wanted to be a Fox anyway!* she thought spitefully.

But no matter how she tried to convince herself that she didn't care, Palmer still felt terrible. She couldn't even enjoy the fact that she had a date with Simmie Randolph.

"Aren't you ecstatic?" Germaine asked one day when Palmer came by for a visit. The older girl was gazing into the mirror, smearing on a green facial mask.

"Soon you'll be seeing the boy of your dreams in person!"

Palmer smiled weakly. "I hope he likes me as much as I like him," she muttered.

"He's going to flip when he sees you in the yellow ski suit!" said Germaine. "How could he not like you? And that thing you thought up about the mystery date is incredible! Simmie must be dying to see what you look like!"

"But suppose he doesn't like the way I look," Palmer said.

Germaine lowered her eyes. "Well, maybe you *should* do something with your hair before the Festival."

"My hair?" Palmer gulped, suddenly worried. "What should I do with it?"

"How about something drastic?" Germaine drawled. "Get one of those punk cuts! I know just the person who could do it!"

"Punk cuts?" said Palmer. "You mean like Amy's?"

"Sure, why not?" Germaine shrugged. "Be daring. Do something different."

"But I'd look terrible like that," said Palmer.

"It was just a suggestion," Germaine said, sounding irritated. She wiped her hands with a tissue.

"How long are you going to leave that stuff on your face?" asked Palmer.

"At least half an hour," Germaine replied, crossing to the bed. "Have you ever tried a beauty mask? You could use one."

"What do you mean?" Palmer frowned. "Is something wrong with my face?"

"Of course not," Germaine said. "Don't be so insecure."

"I'm not insecure," Palmer argued. "It's just that first you said I need a new hairstyle, and now you're telling me I need a beauty mask."

"Sorry," Germaine huffed. "I'm just trying to be helpful. Anyway, I guess you wouldn't want a haircut like your roommate's. It would be odd if the two of you looked alike."

"Amy looks great that way," Palmer blurted out. "It's just that I wouldn't. . . ."

Germaine squinted through the layer of green face cream. Palmer had always liked Germaine's appearance, but with the mask on she was witchy-looking.

"How come you're acting so down?" Germaine muttered. "If I were in your shoes, I'd feel wonderful. Your plan to date Simmie Randolph the Third has worked out perfectly."

"I wish I *could* feel happy about it," groaned Palmer. "But I can't. Amy hates me."

"So what?" Germaine said carelessly.

"I really hurt her feelings," Palmer went on. "I didn't think she'd mind so much. Actually, I didn't think she'd find out."

"That was stupid," Germaine sneered. "Of course she was going to find out someday."

"Well, I didn't know that!" said Palmer.

"What difference does it make anyway?" Germaine said. "You always thought Amy Ho was a weirdo, and you adore Simmie Randolph."

"I really do," gushed Palmer. "I can't stop looking at his picture. But Amy is the one I live with. She's my . . ." Suddenly, Palmer didn't feel like talking to Germaine anymore. It wasn't making her feel better. All the guilt she'd been trying to avoid came flooding in on her. She'd done something really rotten. She couldn't deny that truth any longer. There was only one person in the world she needed to talk to right then. And it wasn't Germaine.

Palmer dashed back to the suite to look for Amy, but Amy wasn't there.

"I think she's down at the river," Shanon said, looking up from her Latin. "She had her skates with her."

"I've got to talk to her," said Palmer. "I guess she's still mad at me, huh?"

"What do *you* think?" Shanon answered quietly.

"I think I'd better go find her," said Palmer. She went into her bedroom, rummaged in the bottom of her trunk for her ice skates, and put on a down parka. Then, fleeing Fox Hall, she headed for the river.

From the top of the hill, Palmer could see that there was only one person on the ice—Amy! She was wearing a red hat with a pom-pom. Probably borrowed it from Lisa, thought Palmer with a smile. Though Amy almost always wore black, Palmer thought she looked nice in the red hat. Then she remembered the silver earmuffs she'd ordered to give Amy as a Christmas present. Her roommate was so mad at her she probably wouldn't even want to accept them.

Trudging down the hill, Palmer stood near the edge of the river. Amy continued to speed along the ice. Palmer was amazed at how smooth and fast she was.

Suddenly, Amy caught sight of her roommate and came to a stop. "What do you want?" she demanded.

"I want to talk to you," Palmer called desperately. "I want to explain things."

Amy glared at her. "There's nothing to explain. Anyway, I'm skating now." And with that, she turned and skated away furiously.

Palmer sat on a bench near the riverbank and hurriedly laced up her skates. Then she glided onto the river and took off after Amy. "You've got to let me explain," she pleaded when she finally caught up to her.

"There's nothing to explain," Amy snapped. Turning to face Palmer, she skated backwards. "You sneaked behind my back and stole my pen pal."

"But I think I really like him!" blurted out Palmer. "And I hated John Adams!"

"Listen to yourself!" Amy exploded. "All you can think about is boys! You never even thought about how you'd be hurting my feelings!"

"You weren't supposed to find out," Palmer said breathlessly. "I didn't even know if Simmie would fall for the mystery Alma girl! Besides, you never seemed all that excited about him."

Amy stopped suddenly. "You still don't get it. I *don't* care a whole lot about Simmie Randolph. He's cute and all that, but I hardly know the guy. His letters aren't especially informative."

"See what I mean?" Palmer said weakly. "I think his letters are nice. And anyway, you wrote to John, didn't you?"

"I can't believe you're even bringing that up!" exclaimed Amy. "You're the one who told me to write him. And I only did it once—to ask about his poem for my song!"

"But don't you see?" Palmer pleaded. "It's all worked out. We can still have pen pals! All four of us! You and I have just switched."

"But you didn't ask to switch," said Amy.

"I did ask in the beginning," Palmer insisted, "when we first started pen pals. And you said you wouldn't."

"If you had asked a second time, I might have changed my mind," Amy said stubbornly. "Anyway, nothing gave you the right to sneak behind our backs like that! As far as Lisa and Shanon and I are concerned, you're a traitor!"

Tears filled Amy's eyes. She didn't want Palmer to see them so she turned and skated away at full speed.

"Wait!" Palmer cried, going after her. "I want to—" But Palmer didn't get a chance to finish the sentence. Suddenly she flew over a bump and lost her balance. Her skates turned inward and then spun out again as she struggled to right herself. "Ouch!" she cried as she fell flat on the ice with one leg twisted beneath her.

Amy looked back over her shoulder and came to a quick stop when she saw Palmer lying there.

"I think I'm hurt," Palmer called weakly.

With a disgusted sigh, Amy skated back to Palmer. "Where does it hurt?' she asked.

Palmer winced in pain. "Right here. I think it's my ankle."

Amy helped her to her feet and over to the riverbank. Then she began to take her skates off.

"How am I going to get back to the dorm?" Palmer whimpered.

"Don't worry," Amy said, putting on one of her boots. "I'll get you up there."

"Thanks," said Palmer gratefully. "It feels like my ankle's sprained pretty badly. I guess you wish I'd broken my neck instead, huh?"

Amy frowned. "Why would I wish something dumb like that?"

"I don't know," Palmer said. "Because you hate me."

Amy grinned a little. "Oh, yeah, that's right, I do." And reaching out, she helped Palmer up. "Put your arm on my shoulder," she directed.

"Are you sure?" Palmer asked.

"Don't worry," Amy said, "I'm strong enough. Here, lean on me. . . ."

CHAPTER SIXTEEN

"Look!" Shanon cried out on the morning of Winter Festival. "Some of the Ardsley buses are already here!" She pulled Lisa over to the sitting-room window. Amy, Brenda, and Kate were on the loveseat quietly going over Brenda's song. Palmer was in the bedroom, still sleeping.

"How many boys from Ardsley are coming?" Lisa asked, looking out the window. "I saw one bus already parked on the other side of the quadrangle."

"I think it's going to be a big turnout," Kate called over her strumming. She'd agreed to perform Amy's song with Brenda, but they hadn't had much time to practice.

Shanon rushed over to the mirror. She was already dressed in pink ski pants and a white parka. "Do I look okay?" she asked nervously. "I'm supposed to meet Mars in five minutes. I wonder which one of those buses he came on."

"What did you sign up for this morning?" Lisa asked, trying to sound cheerful. "Tobogganing or cross-country skiing?"

Shanon ran a brush through her hair. "Cross-country," she replied breathlessly.

Lisa turned away.

"I'm sorry Rob's not coming," Shanon said softly.

"It's my own fault," Lisa muttered. "At least I cleared up that business about the paper with Mr. Griffith. I saw him just now in his office and he really liked this last one."

"The one from your own experience?" Amy asked, overhearing.

Lisa nodded.

"That's great," said Shanon. She gave Lisa a hug and headed for the doorway. "Well, I guess I'll see you all around somewhere today. Good luck on your Talent Night number, Brenda! I'll be there!"

Squashed between Amy and Kate, Brenda sat rigid on the loveseat. "I'll be there, too," she said, her voice quavering.

As Shanon headed out the door, Amy turned her attention again to Kate and Brenda.

"What do you think?" Brenda asked. "Am I going to sound all right?"

"You'll both be fine," said Amy. "Just don't let it drag, and remember not to come in too early after the break."

"I've got to go," said Kate. "I'm late already."

"Just one more time," begged Brenda.

"All right," Kate said, impatiently. "But that will have to be it until this evening. I've . . . got to go somewhere."

"That's right, you have a date, don't you?" Lisa said, putting on her mittens.

Kate turned scarlet. "I'm supposed to be meeting some-body."

"Well, at least you and Shanon have boys to do things with," Lisa said. She forced a smile. "I'm still going to have a go at the snow sculpture, though."

"Good luck," said Amy.

Lisa grinned. "Thanks." She eyed the closed door to the bedroom. "How's Palmer?" she whispered. "You think she'll be okay if we all leave her?"

"I'll look in on her before I go for the skating event," Amy said.

"I guess she's pretty depressed," Brenda piped up. "It's really bad luck that she sprained her ankle and has to miss everything."

Lisa shrugged. "Bad luck for her. But maybe not for you, Amy. I mean . . . Simmie Randolph is probably still going to be there. You could . . ."

Amy gave Lisa a warning look. "I told you I don't want to talk about him."

"Suit yourself," said Lisa. "But he's going to be all by himself now. I'd better get out of here. I'm roasting in this snow suit." She hit Amy's hand with her mitten. "See you later! And try to have fun. I'm going to. Maybe I'll even run into my brother Reggie. I don't know if he was planning to come to this—"

"Oh, he is!" Kate blurted.

Lisa turned in the doorway and gave Kate a questioning look.

"I think he might be sledding today," Kate murmured.

"Thanks!" Lisa said cheerfully. "I'll check it out!"

Brenda, Amy, and Kate were left alone.

"I really don't think there's any point in going over the song again," Kate said, getting up. "And anyway I have to go."

"What event are you doing?" Amy asked curiously.

Kate blushed again. "Sledding."

104

Amy's eyes lit up. "Just like Reggie McGreevy, huh? How come you knew Lisa's brother was coming today?"

"Because . . . because I do, that's all," Kate stammered. She grabbed her guitar picks. "I've really got to go now."

"Thanks for everything," Brenda called.

"No problem," replied Kate. "Don't be so nervous. You'll do fine tonight."

Brenda sighed. "I hope so."

Kate shut the door behind her.

"I've got to warm up for the skating event," Amy said apologetically. "Your voice sounds great. Kate's right. You shouldn't worry."

"But I've never performed in public before," Brenda protested. "Couldn't we just go over the song one more time? It's not my voice I'm worried about. It's those new lyrics. Is the guy who wrote the chorus going to be here tonight?"

"I don't think so," said Amy. She smiled patiently. "Okay, we'll do it one more time. But after this, you're through rehearsing. There comes a point when you just have to wing it."

Settling on the loveseat, Amy strummed the familiar chords to her song. Brenda's clear voice gave the lyrics a haunting quality. The door to Palmer and Amy's bedroom opened softly and Palmer stood listening. Her ankle was tightly bandaged and she was on crutches. Turning, Amy signaled Brenda to stop.

"Don't stop," Palmer said. "I mean . . . it's okay. You're not bothering me."

Amy rested her guitar. "We're done, anyway. Right, Brenda?"

"Right," Brenda replied bravely. She got up to leave. "Good luck in the skating race!"

"Thanks," Amy called after her. "See you later!"

Palmer hobbled out into the room. Her face looked pale and she was still in her nightgown.

"You slept a long time," Amy said. "Mrs. Butter sent you some breakfast."

"Wow," Palmer said. "And you brought it all the way back for me? I hope it's not oatmeal," she added suspiciously.

"It's only a bagel and orange juice." Amy grinned. "Mrs. Butter says it'll 'stick to your ribs, love!' "

Palmer smiled. "Except for the fact that we'd all weigh a ton if she had her way, Mrs. Butter is really okay."

"She certainly takes good care of us," said Amy as she helped Palmer settle into a chair. "Want a pillow to prop your foot up?"

"Thanks," Palmer said meekly. "And can I have the orange juice also?"

"Sure." Amy propped up Palmer's leg and then gave her a carton of orange juice, a napkin, and the bagel. "Anything else?"

Palmer sighed. "No, this is great. Thanks."

Amy started for the bedroom. "Well, I'm going to get ready now."

"Wait!" Palmer called. "I was going to . . . well, I was wondering if you wanted my new ski suit. I mean, I won't be needing it today."

"You *could* wear it yourself," Amy reminded her. "Just because you can't go skiing doesn't mean you can't watch some of the other events."

106

Palmer shook her head. "No, I don't want to. I only wanted to do the skiing. Anyway, you can have the ski suit."

"I've got my vest," said Amy. "Thanks anyway."

Palmer cleared her throat. "I'm the one who ought to be thanking you," she said quietly. "I feel sort of awful. After what I did to you, you're being so nice to me."

"It was bad luck that you sprained your ankle. If it had been me, you'd help me out, too, right?"

"I . . . I guess I would," said Palmer. She swallowed and tried to feel sincere. But somehow in the bottom of her heart, she knew she probably wouldn't be as nice as Amy was being. "If you want to see Simmie," she offered suddenly, "I'll tell you where he's going to be."

"Where?" Amy asked curiously.

"He was going to meet 'P'—that is, me—at ten o'clock at the bottom of the downhill ski trail," she said quickly. "He was going to know I was his mystery date because I'd be wearing a yellow ski suit."

"Neat trick," Amy said flatly. She pulled on her vest and grabbed her skates. "I don't think I'll play it, though."

"Good luck in the race," Palmer said. "Oh, I almost forgot. I have something for you."

"For me?" Amy asked in surprise.

Palmer got up and hobbled to the desk. In the top drawer were the silver earmuffs.

"Wow," Amy said with a grin. "They're cool." She looked at Palmer for a moment. "I'll wear them for good luck, okay?"

"That would be great," said Palmer. "I ordered them the same time that Germaine and I . . ." Her voice trailed off.

"Germaine didn't happen to come by while I was asleep?" she asked nonchalantly.

"I haven't seen her," Amy replied, pulling her gloves on.

"I guess she's busy," Palmer hedged. "Germaine's got three boyfriends, you know!"

"Good for her," muttered Amy. "Listen, I'll check in on you later. If you get dressed, we can walk over to lunch. Those crutches work, you know."

"I know," Palmer said glumly. Amy put on her silver earmuffs, slung her skates over one shoulder, and strode out the door.

As soon as she was alone, Palmer's spirits sunk even lower. This had to be the most miserable day of her life! Simmie Randolph III was going to be waiting for her in person, and she wasn't going to be there. And on top of that she'd wrecked Amy's chances of having a date for the Festival. Amy was being a good sport, but underneath it all, Palmer knew she'd lost a friend. And then there was Germaine. She seemed to have forgotten that Palmer was even alive! Palmer had to be the unhappiest person on the whole planet!

Hobbling over to the window, she peeked out at the bright and glorious day. She pulled down the shade and sighed. So much for Winter Festival. . . .

CHAPTER SEVENTEEN

———◆———

The air outside was cold and clear as crystal. The limbs of the trees were coated with shimmering frost and giant icicles sparkled in the sun. *What a perfect day*, thought Shanon. Her whole body tingled with anticipation at what was to come. First, she'd go cross-country skiing, her favorite winter sport. Then she was going to the Brier Mountain slope to watch the Alma/Ardsley downhill ski exhibition so she could write something about it for *The Ledger*. But best of all—she was going to see her pen pal! Any minute, she would see Mars!

As she neared the cross-country area, her knees suddenly felt like jelly. *Not a very good condition to be in if you're going to ski,* she thought, laughing at herself. It was amazing how nervous and happy and scared she was at the thought of meeting Mars again.

It had been over two months since they'd seen each other, and that was only for a short while at the Halloween dance. At least she had his picture, Shanon thought. At least she'd have no problem recognizing him. Now if only she could think of something to talk about to him and not come off sounding boring. When she wrote her letters, she had time to decide what she wanted to tell him. And writing had never been hard for Shanon; but talking to someone face to face was another story altogether.

Dozens of Ardsley boys were already milling around the cross-country area in parkas of various colors. Some were with Alma girls, others in groups by themselves. Shanon caught sight of Dolores in a big fur hat; she was stepping onto her skis while a tall boy from Ardsley held her poles for her. Shanon waved.

"Get a good story!" Dolores called gaily. She smiled at the boy standing next to her; he handed her her poles and they whooshed off together. Dolores always seemed so confident, thought Shanon. Of course she'd probably done lots of dating. She was three years older than Shanon. Being twelve and shy, Shanon was still pretty inexperienced with boys. In fact, this was her first real date—and all thanks to the fact that she had an Ardsley pen pal.

After picking up her skis and poles, she stood away from the crowd to wait for Mars. *Maybe he's decided not to come,* she thought, squinting into the sunlight.

Suddenly a boy in a red parka came striding toward her. He had a bright blue bandana tied around his forehead and his face was sunburned. He stuck out one of his hands. He was wearing blue ski gloves.

"Hey, Shanon!"

Shanon swallowed. "Mars?" She stuck out her own white-mittened hand. He looked so much more handsome than she had remembered, so much better than in that fuzzy picture. And his hair seemed longer. It was sticking out from under his ski cap. They shook hands for a long time. Shanon caught her breath and looked down. Mars began getting into his skis.

"I don't know about you, but I'm ready to take off," he said abruptly.

"Oh, I am, too," Shanon replied, flushing. She bent down to secure her skis. "How's your pen-holder business?" she asked, making small talk.

"It's great," he answered. "That reminds me. I brought one for you. I'll give it to you later." He paused awkwardly. "How's your work on the newspaper?"

"Fantastic," she replied. "I have to do a story on some of the events. I hope you don't mind."

"Heck no," Mars said. "I'll go with you. Where do you have to be?"

"At the downhill exhibition," she explained. "I thought that maybe . . ." She stood up and caught him staring at her. His eyes were just as dark as she remembered, just as intense-looking.

"Maybe what?" he asked, looking away again.

"Maybe, uh, we could go over to Brier on our skis," she said shyly. "That is, if you want to. There's a trail through the woods. It's only a couple of miles from here."

"Sounds good! Let's get going."

"Okay!" cried Shanon, pushing off. She entered the snowy woods with Mars closely following. The only sounds were the swooshing of their skis on the powdery, white trail and the faint laughter of other skiers further up the trail.

"This is great," Mars said softly, coming up beside Shanon. "Sort of an enchanted forest." He smiled and Shanon's heart pounded.

111

"You look a little different," she said, gulping. "I mean . . . your hair, it's longer."

"So is yours," Mars said quickly. "I mean, of course yours is really long. I just need a haircut. Anyway . . . thanks for inviting me."

Shanon's cheeks burned as she smiled back at him. "Thanks for coming." So far her very first date felt like a dream.

Across the campus, Lisa dug her shovel deep into the snow. Even though she was on her own, she was determined to make her snowperson sculpture. Of course it wouldn't be quite as abominable as it would have been with Rob's help. It wouldn't be as large either. But she was still going to enter the competition.

She spritzed the beginning of her sculpture and studied the base, not sure how to proceed. Oh well, at least nobody really knew what the Abominable Snowperson looked like. That meant no matter how it turned out, it would be okay. Lisa actually had a pretty clear idea of what she wanted. She wondered if Rob had agreed with it. He'd never had a chance to write back about her drawing.

Suddenly, she heard a strange growling sound behind her. She spun around and saw a figure in furry boots and mittens and a white woolen ski mask. The figure began growling again. Lisa knew it was just someone kidding around, but it was still a little scary.

"Cut it out," she said irritably. "Who are you?"

"The Abominable Snowperson," the figure growled.

Lisa stood up with her hands on her hips. "What? . . . Who?"

The bulky mittens clumsily peeled off the ski mask, and

112

a good-looking boy with a mop of dark, curly hair stood looking at her. Lisa's mouth fell open. "Rob? Is that you?"

"Who'd you think it was?" Rob answered. "Mr. Abominable?"

Lisa's face got red. "You decided to come, huh?"

"Winter Festival is a big event," Rob said casually.

Lisa picked up her shovel again. "Yeah, I guess you wouldn't want to miss it," she mumbled.

Rob shuffled his feet for a minute. "Look, Lisa . . ."

"Yes?" she said eagerly. It was so great to see him!

"Nothing," he muttered. "See you later!"

"Wait!" Lisa said. "I want to apologize."

"I want to apologize, too."

"No, I'm the one who accused you of getting me in trouble," she said.

"But I gave you a bad idea," Rob insisted.

Lisa smiled at him. "It turned out okay, though. Mr. Griffith gave me another chance and I wrote something from my own life experience. I wrote about that time I got lost when I was little."

"I'd like to read it," Rob said quickly. "I mean . . ." He looked down at his boots. "I've missed your letters. We were really getting to . . . know each other."

Lisa felt her face flush. She had never stopped liking Rob even when she was mad at him.

"Are you still entering the sculpture competition?" he asked.

"Doing the Abominable Snowperson," Lisa said brightly. They both reached for the shovel and touched mittens. Lisa felt a charge. She wondered if it was something coming from Rob or just static electricity.

"I'm glad you're still doing it," Rob said quietly. "I

113

thought your drawing was sensational. Can I do it with you?" His eyes were dark blue like an ocean.

Lisa smiled. "Sure, if you want to."

"All right!" Rob yelled, letting go of the shovel. "Let's scoop some snow!"

Rob got down on the ground and Lisa knelt next to him. Her heart turned over as they thrust their hands into the snow and laughed.

CHAPTER EIGHTEEN

Amy's heart sang as she cut through the ice on the river. The wind burned her face and tore at her hair. The temperature was getting lower, but she didn't notice. Her whole being was involved in the effort of getting to the finish. There were over twenty entrants in the speed competition. Trees and other skaters flashed by as she strained to catch the lead pack. It was almost as if she were flying. The finish line was a red streak of ribbon just in front of her. She crossed with the first group. She was sixth!

"Nice going!" A tall, gawky-looking boy with red hair caught her at the sideline.

"Thanks," Amy gasped.

"Can I walk you over to the shelter?" the boy asked.

Amy stopped and gave him a puzzled look. He was acting as if he knew her. "Sure," she said with a grin. "You're the only one here to congratulate me."

The boy's face flushed. "I wouldn't have missed it," he told her. "Actually, somebody in the crowd pointed you out to me. You were so outstanding, I wondered who you were."

Amy smiled. "Thanks again. Do we . . . ? We don't know each other, do we? I mean . . . you must be from Ardsley."

They walked toward the shelter. The boy's light brown eyes twinkled mischievously. "We do sort of know each other," he explained. "In fact, you could say we're collaborators."

Amy stepped into the shelter, where one of the coaches gave her a towel and something to drink. Coach Haig appeared and put an arm around her. "Good work, Ho," she said proudly.

"Thanks, Mrs. Haig," Amy replied, flushing with victory.

The red-haired boy stuck his hand out. "You must be Coach Haig! I've heard that your soccer team this year was one of the best in the league."

"Thanks, young man," Mrs. Haig said, shaking his hand warmly. She turned to Amy. "Aren't you going to introduce me to your friend, Amy?"

"I . . . I don't know . . ." Amy giggled in embarrassment. Turning to the boy she said, "What *is* your name?"

"I thought you might have guessed it," he chuckled. "John Adams."

"John Adams!" she exclaimed. "I'm sorry . . . I mean . . . I didn't recognize you. This is John Adams, Mrs. Haig," she said quickly.

Mrs. Haig smiled. "Glad to meet you, young man. Enjoy the weekend! Make sure you cool down before you go out again, Amy."

The coach walked away, leaving Amy and John staring at each other. "I feel really dumb," Amy said. "I've seen your picture, but I guess I forgot what you look like."

"Why should you remember?" he said, shrugging. Amy noticed how intelligent John's eyes were. His hair was an unusual shade of red and very thick.

"I *am* using your poem for my song," she offered apologetically. "The least I can do is recognize my collaborator when I see him."

He laughed quietly. "I wasn't supposed to be coming. Remember?"

"I remember," she said awkwardly. "Palmer . . ."

"Palmer disinvited me, so to speak," John said, finishing the thought.

"That was kind of mean," Amy said. "I'm sorry she did that. I hope it didn't hurt your feelings."

"It did hurt my feelings," John said bluntly. "But then I decided I wasn't going to let that stop me from hearing your song."

"Wow," Amy said. "Is that why you decided to come?"

"That's the reason," he replied. He stared at her face and smiled again. "You're a really neat-looking person," he told her.

Amy shrugged. "Thanks."

"I remember when you sent that picture to my roommate I thought the same thing."

"That's right—Simmie shares a room with you." She stuck her hands into her pockets. "I guess you heard that, uh, well . . ." She looked down.

"Hey, it's nothing to be embarrassed about," John said, touching her shoulder gently. "We both sort of got dumped, I guess. But Palmer and Simmie were only our pen pals, right?"

"Yeah, sure . . ." Amy tried to shrug off her embarrassment. "It was nothing. Well, I guess I'm ready to get out of here."

"Me too," he said, zipping up his parka. "I like your earmuffs."

Amy laughed. "They're my good luck . . . from Palmer."

They looked at each other awkwardly.

"Mind if I hang out with you for a while?" John asked suddenly. "I mean, unless you have other plans."

"I was going to catch a toboggan ride," Amy said.

"Great, I love tobogganing," he said enthusiastically. "Is the trail over near Brier? I want to catch the downhill, too. My roommate—" He broke off abruptly and looked at his feet.

"It's okay to mention Simmie," Amy said good-naturedly, leading him out of the shelter. "To tell you the truth, I never was too hot on his letters. I guess he doesn't like to write much."

"Actually, it's his spelling that's the problem," John said, smothering a laugh.

Amy giggled. "Right, he wasn't much of a speller."

There was a van outside waiting to take a load of passengers over to Brier. Amy and John ran toward it. It was a tight squeeze, but they both managed to get seats.

"By the way," John said, looking straight ahead, "where *is* Palmer?"

"Oh, I guess you haven't heard," Amy answered. "She hurt her ankle."

"I hope it's nothing too bad," John said.

Amy sunk her chin down into her muffler. "No, she's okay. She just won't be doing any skiing this weekend."

Even though the van was stuffy, the ride to Brier was

fun. Everybody seemed to be in high spirits. Amy hadn't been expecting to spend the day with John Adams, but she was glad for the opportunity. Ever since she'd read his poem, she'd wondered what kind of person he was.

The toboggan ride was wonderful. Amy sat in a crush with John and six other people. When that was over, they ran into Shanon and Mars at the downhill.

"Has Simmie gone yet?" John asked Mars.

"He's next," Mars answered. Amy grabbed Shanon's field glasses. Simmie stood poised at the top of the run. He was dressed in a brilliant blue parka and his hair shone golden in the sunlight.

She gave the glasses back to Shanon. "Did you see him?" Shanon whispered.

"Yeah, he looks great," Amy said glumly. Even at a distance, Simmie looked as good as his poster. And to think he had once been her pen pal.

"There he goes!" Mars shouted excitedly. Simmie did a breathtaking spread eagle with a perfect landing. The spectators cheered and applauded wildly as he sped down the hill.

"He's a fantastic athlete," John said agreeably.

"Hey, who's that?" Shanon said, peering through the glasses. She passed them to Amy. "Take a look."

Down at the bottom of the hill Simmie was being congratulated by a girl in a bright yellow ski suit.

"That must be 'P'—Simmie's mystery date!" Mars chortled. "She's really wearing a yellow ski suit!"

"But it can't be Palmer!" exclaimed Shanon.

John's face clouded. "Palmer? Why would it be her?"

"I'll explain later," Amy said hurriedly. "Right now, I've

got to go talk to someone." And she headed briskly toward the finish line.

The girl in the yellow ski suit had her back to Amy, but she was all over Simmie, brushing snow off his parka and giggling flirtatiously. Amy stopped and tapped the girl on the shoulder.

"Germaine!" Amy exclaimed when the girl turned around.

"Oh, hi," Germaine replied unenthusiastically. "Can I help you?"

Simmie flashed a smile. "Hi, Amy."

She glared at him. "Hi, yourself."

Simmie smiled at Germaine and then back at Amy again as if he didn't know what to do. For a super-handsome guy, Amy thought, he suddenly looked pretty goofy.

"Wasn't Simmie wonderful in the exhibition?" Germaine said, linking her arm through Simmie's as if they were already good friends.

"I'm sorry about that letter I wrote you," Simmie said uncomfortably. He looked at Germaine sheepishly and shrugged his shoulders. "But you know . . . well, maybe you don't know . . ."

"I know all right," Amy said. She gave Germaine a hard glare. "Could I speak with Simmie alone for a moment?"

"I don't know," Germaine huffed. "We were going to take a walk or something."

"You heard me, Germaine," Amy said threateningly. "Unless you want to have a snowball under your hat, get lost!"

Germaine gave Amy a dirty look, then smiled at Simmie. "I'll be back in a minute!" she assured him. "Don't take too long," she hissed at Amy before stalking off.

120

Amy and Simmie were left staring at each other.

"I hope you're not mad at me," Simmie said, shifting uncomfortably from foot to foot. "I know that letter I wrote was mean."

"It was mean all right," Amy said angrily. She glared in Germaine's direction. "But that's not what I want to talk to you about. . . ."

"This is really nice of you, Amy!" Palmer said as she stood looking into her bedroom closet that evening. Her roommate had just offered to help her over to the assembly hall for Talent Night.

"Will you hurry?" Amy urged, glancing at her watch.

"I can't decide which sweater to wear," Palmer said. "The yellow matches my hair, but the blue matches my eyes. Or maybe I should just wear my tweed pants suit with a white blouse."

Amy rolled her eyes. "I think your yellow sweater will be great. And you can't change pants again. It takes too long with your ankle."

"Whatever you say!" Palmer said brightly. Pulling on her yellow sweater, she looked in the mirror and fluffed her silky blonde hair. "Are Shanon and Lisa going over with us?" she asked.

"Yes," said Amy, getting her coat. "And we can't be late because my song is near the beginning!"

"Oh, your song, that's right," Palmer said, giggling. "I'd almost forgotten why we were going."

They left the suite, Palmer hobbling down the stairs with Amy right behind her. Shanon and Lisa were waiting with a group in the common room.

"Hi, everybody!" Palmer called gaily. The group turned

around, and the first face she saw belonged to John Adams. "Hi," she said in a quieter voice, blushing. She turned to Amy. "Why didn't you tell me he was here?" she whispered. "This is too embarrassing."

"Cool your jets," Amy whispered back, smiling. "He's *my* date."

"*Your* date?"

Simmie stepped out of the group and walked toward them. "Hey Palmer," he said, flashing a big smile. "I heard about your ankle. I'm really sorry."

"Thanks," she said. "Would somebody please tell me what's going on?" She giggled nervously.

"We thought we'd all go to the Talent Night," Lisa announced for Palmer's benefit. "The Foxes and the Unknowns together—though not exactly the way we planned it."

Palmer's face fell. "You mean ... because of what I did," she said quietly. "If this is your way of humiliating me ..."

"Nobody's trying to humiliate anybody," John reassured her. "We just thought you'd like a mystery date."

Simmie chortled. "It was a pretty good trick! A good thing Amy told me it was you. I was about to go off with some *other* girl in a yellow ski suit!"

Everyone laughed and Palmer smiled. "I still don't understand," she said sweetly.

"We'll tell you later on," Amy said. "Now, let's go hear my song!"

John grabbed Amy's arm. "Our song, you mean! 'Cabin Fever!' "

As they walked over to the assembly hall, they became

part of a bigger and bigger crowd. Amy felt herself getting nervous. "I'd better go backstage and make sure Brenda and Kate are okay," she announced.

"I'll grab some seats down front," John said. "Tell them to break a leg!"

"Speaking of legs, maybe we'd better sit in the back," Simmie suggested to Palmer.

"Great," Palmer said breathlessly. "If we can get an aisle seat, I won't have to climb over everyone."

"Look!" Lisa exclaimed, scanning the audience. "There's my English teacher with my French teacher! Don't they look incredibly cute?"

Rob caught sight of Miss Grayson and Mr. Griffith standing near the door. "They look nice," he agreed. When Mr. Griffith put his arm around Miss Grayson, Rob laughed. "They also look like they like each other."

Lisa blushed and giggled. She wondered if Rob would try to put his arm around her when the lights went down.

"Hey, sis!" Lisa turned and saw her brother Reggie standing behind her. He was wearing a blue blazer and looked thinner than ever.

"Reggie," she exclaimed, giving him a hug. "How come you're here?"

"I have a date," he mumbled shyly. "I mean . . . there's this girl playing the guitar in the show."

"Who?" Lisa asked.

"Her name is Kate," he replied uncomfortably.

Lisa shrieked. "Kate Majors? You've got to be kidding! I mean that's nice," she added, trying to control herself. Of all the girls at Alma, her brother had to pick Kate Majors! Even though Kate was Shanon's friend, Lisa thought the girl was much too bossy. She didn't like the idea of Kate and Reggie going together. But for the moment she decided not to say anything. . . .

"I'm going up front to get a good view," Reggie said, flushing.

"Let's sit down," Mars suggested. He grabbed Shanon's arm and they scooted past Rob and Lisa. "Here's that little thing I promised you," Mars whispered, once they were seated. Shanon giggled as he reached into his pocket and handed over a pen wrapped in a pen holder.

Rob and Lisa had finally taken the seats on the aisle, with Palmer and Simmie right behind them. John had saved a seat down front for Amy, who returned just as the lights were dimming.

"Is everything okay with the performers?" John whispered.

"They seem fine," Amy answered, settling in. "It's me who's nervous."

He squeezed her hand. "Me, too. After all, it's our first collaboration."

Amy felt her head spin. There was definitely something terrific about John Adams. And it wasn't just the way he looked.

CHAPTER NINETEEN

———◆———

Dear Palmer,
   It was deelightful to see you at the Festival and that was
an understatement. Have you ever heard the expression
race my motor? Ha, ha, you race mine. By the way, I can't
wait to see your car. Perhaps we can arrange it over spring
vacation. This brake I am not going back to Florida. The
family is getting together in the Bahamas. Look foreward
to writing to you about your hobbies and other things.
                                                    Simmie
P.S. What are your hobbies anyway?

Dear Shanon,
   There's not much to say since we just saw each other,
except that I came down with a cold as soon as I got back.
But it was worth it. It's going to be strange breaking for
the holiday, because I won't be here to get a letter from
you. I really look forward to them. But mostly I look
forward to you. Let's get your headmistress to sponsor

another weekend soon. In the meantime, send me a copy of your ski article.

> Yours truly,
> Mars

P.S. I'll be thinking of you the night of the Winter Solstice.

Dear Lisa,

Wasn't that snowperson abominable? We may not have won any prizes, but it was really fun. I enjoyed it. Especially the next day when we got together in the common room.

Have you ever played the game Truth or Consequences? The Unknowns have their own version of it. The other day when Arthur (Shanon may call him Mars, but I call him by his real name) asked me what was really on my mind, all I could say was "Lisa." I'm glad we made up. Write to me.

> Rob, your pen pal forever

P.S. Tell Amy Ho I think she did a good job with that song she wrote. It was also great hearing John's poetry in the lyrics.

Dear Amy,

I had an amazing time at the Festival. I'm really glad things worked out the way they did. I would also like for you to be my pen pal. We have a lot to write about. Hope you say yes.

> John Adams

P.S. Send me a copy of the song. You're a good musician. By the way, when I was sitting next to you at the Talent Night, I thought maybe I "found the answer."

"Are you going to answer yours right away?" Lisa asked excitedly.

Shanon poured some water from the new teapot. "I'm going to write to Mars tonight," she said, blushing.

"I'm going to write to Simmie, too!" said Palmer. "I wonder what he means by hobbies?"

"You know what a hobby is," teased Amy. "Something you do with your spare time."

"Like order clothes from catalogues," quipped Lisa.

"Come on!" wailed Palmer. "I can't write that down. I guess I'll just have to work on developing some hobbies, that's all."

"Good idea," said Shanon. "What about pottery or carpentry or playing the piano?"

Palmer sighed. "It makes me tired just to think about that kind of stuff. Pass me some tea, will you?"

Shanon brought a mug over. "Your own special mug, compliments of Lisa!"

"These are nice," said Palmer.

"And isn't the teapot she made for Shanon neat?" Amy added.

"Thanks," Lisa said, smiling. "I wanted to finish up my pottery projects before the holidays. Of course I still haven't finished my history paper."

Amy laughed. "Oh, well, you can't finish everything!"

"You're in a good mood," Palmer said. "Is it because of your letter from John?"

Amy nodded. "Yes. I think I'll definitely keep him as a pen pal."

"Great!" said Lisa.

Palmer smiled triumphantly. "You see! Everything

worked out fine! And it was all because of that idea I had for the mystery date!"

"Well, that's one way of looking at it," Lisa said doubtfully.

"But it still wasn't very honest of you," Shanon chimed in.

Palmer flashed a smile. "Amy thinks it's okay now. Don't you, Amy?"

Amy raised an eyebrow. "It worked out okay *this* time. But I hope you don't ever pull anything underhanded like that again."

"I won't, I promise," Palmer said sincerely.

"Anyway," Amy admitted, "I never did have much in common with Simmie Randolph. I just thought he was good-looking."

"He's *so* good looking!" Palmer gushed. "It was nice of you to set me up with him at Talent Night," she added.

"Well, I couldn't see Germaine cashing in like that," said Amy.

"Imagine her trying to pass herself off as Simmie's mystery date!" Lisa exclaimed.

Shanon sighed. "Some people are so low."

"Germaine did turn out to be a witch," Palmer admitted. "She told me she had three boyfriends when all the time she didn't have a single one!"

"It's no wonder!" Lisa said. "Only someone with mental problems would see anything in Germaine Richards!"

Amy elbowed Lisa and glanced at Palmer.

"It's okay," Palmer said. "I guess I was just bowled over by the fact that someone as sophisticated as Germaine wanted to hang out with me. But she was no friend of mine. And all along I couldn't see that you guys were the ones who really . . . you know . . . the ones . . ." She got misty for a moment as she looked at the three other Foxes.

Amy came over and patted Palmer's shoulder. "It's okay, Durand," she said with a grin. "We know you like us."

"I really do," Palmer blurted out, looking embarrassed. "I mean . . . sometimes it takes a while to figure out who your real friends are."

Amy and Palmer gave each other a little hug. Then Shanon poured everyone more tea.

"I can't wait to get home and pump Reggie about his date with Kate," Lisa said gaily. "To think that my brother would go with someone as bossy as that! I bet the two of them are writing letters back and forth just like we are with The Unknown. I'd give anything to know what they write to each other."

"Curiosity killed the cat," Shanon warned. "You'd better not interfere with Reggie and Kate."

"I guess you're right," grumbled Lisa. "I won't say a word about her when Reggie and I get home."

"I can't wait to see Mom and Dad and my sister Doreen," chirped Shanon. "And my Uncle Bill and Aunt Gloria and cousin Charles and—"

"Somebody stop her!" shrieked Lisa. "We'll be here all night listening to the names of all the people in that family!"

"I can't wait to see my parents and grandmother, too," Amy called, heading off to her room.

"I guess I'll be glad to see my mother," Palmer added, following. "But I'll miss . . . everybody here."

Amy stopped in the doorway and looked at Palmer, and Palmer looked at Lisa and Lisa at Shanon. "I guess we'll all miss each other," Lisa said. "When we come back it'll be a new year."

"But . . ." Shanon added with a smile, "we'll still be the Foxes!" The four girls came together into a bear hug.

Dear Simmie,

I too had a deelightful time at the Winter Festival. I was afraid at first that my roommate Amy would be mad at me, because we switched pen pals. But she isn't. Thought you'd like to know that. I look forward to writing you about all kinds of things in the new year. And to seeing you sometimes, too.

Yours truly,
Palmer Durand

P.S. I have to talk to you about my car sometime. I don't exactly have it yet. Also, what do you mean by hobbies? Are there any that you think are better than others?

Dear Mars,

Thank you for your letter and for the pen holder which I use all the time. Especially when I am about to write a letter! Lisa, Amy, and Palmer also want personal pen holders.

I had a wonderful time seeing you. My article will not come out until after the holidays, but I'll send a copy of it to you then.

I was thinking about the Winter Solstice. It is nice of you to say you'll be thinking of me. I will try to imagine where you are on that night, too. The neat thing is that wherever we are, when we look up, we will see the same stars.

This comes with best wishes for a magical new year.

Your pen pal,
Shanon Davis

130

Dear Rob,

You signed your letter "your pen pal forever." That was really nice of you. Wouldn't it be amazing to write to somebody for ten or fifteen years? A lot would happen. Sometimes I don't want to think about it, because that would mean that I would be really old. Or maybe both of us would live in other places that we don't even imagine. That might be fun! But I don't know about the old part, except that my grandmother Gammy says that being old is great. Anyway, I will never forget the time we had together at the Festival and I look forward to writing after the holidays.

Your pen pal "forever,"
Lisa

Dear John,

It was the greatest, sitting there listening to our song. Who knows, maybe "Cabin Fever" will be on the charts. The audience sure liked it. And it gave Brenda a lot of confidence.

To answer your question, I would like to be your pen pal. When you say maybe we've "found the answer," I say maybe you're right. When I heard Brenda singing our song on stage, it was like something broke through inside of me. So now maybe even if I am cooped up here surrounded by snow I won't feel so restless. Here's the copy of the song you asked for.

CABIN FEVER
Song by Amy Ho;
Lyrics by Amy Ho and John Adams

The day dawns
my heart is breaking, breaking like the sun
cause of—
CABIN FEVER!
I'm aching, aching to have fun
Oh, CABIN FEVER!
Have you ever felt that way? like your ship came in to stay
When the tide came rushing to enchanted borders?
Oh, cabin fever!
I've got it! My temperature's a hundred and four!
What is the cure—
For cabin fever?
Where is the answer?

CHORUS:
Just run a mile through acid rain
And write down our life's story
Emblaze your name upon my brain
Cool your fiery hands with snow . . .
Oh, cabin fever!
We've found the answer!
Oh, cabin fever!

Happy New Year.

Your new pen pal,
Amy

P.S. The answer is not just in writing songs; it's in writing letters. Let's do it!

HAPPY HOLIDAYS TO THE ARDSLEY UNKNOWN
ROBBIE WILLIAMS, ARTHUR "MARS" MARTINEZ,
SIMMIE RANDOLPH III, AND JOHN ADAMS
FROM THE FOXES OF THE THIRD DIMENSION
LISA MCGREEVY, SHANON DAVIS, PALMER
DURAND, AND AMY HO!
AND GOOD WRITING IN THE NEW YEAR!